Some reviews of Jiggy McCue Books

The Poltergoose
Shortlisted for the Blue Peter Book Award
"A laugh a minute. I couldn't stop turning the pages!"
Caroline, age 12

"A mix of sitcom farce and hardboiled American detective novel.
The book's climax – the reburial of a goose with a restless
spirit – features a hilarious sequence in a ladies toilet."
Michael Thorn, *Times Educational Supplement*

The Killer Underpants
Winner of the Stockton Children's Book of the Year Award
"...the funniest book I've ever read."
Teen Titles

"Very funny, pretty rude, and sometimes revolting!"
Lorraine Orman, *Story-Go-Round*

The Toilet of Doom
"Fast, furious and full of good humour."
National Literacy Association

Maggot Pie
"Will have you squirming with horror and delight!"
Ottakars 8-12 Book of the Month

"Funny, wacky and lively."
cool-reads.co.uk

The Snottle
"Awesome!"
5 Star Amazon review by Charlie, age 10

Nudie Dudie
Winner of the Doncaster Children's Book Award
Winner of the Solihull Children's Book Award
Highly Commended for the Sheffield Children's Book Award
"Fantastic! Will make you giggle and laugh till it hurts
you so bad you start jumping up and down."
5 Star Amazon review by Kaz, age 13

About this book

KID SWAP is the tenth Jiggy McCue book, and it's an unusual one because it wasn't intended to be a book at all, but just one story among several told by Jiggy, Angie, Pete and Jig's aggressive cat, Stallone. However, the story grew and grew, and it soon became clear that it had to be a novel in its own right rather than part of another book. And here it is. Hope you like it. The story collection (minus Kid Swap) will now be the eleventh in the series. It will be called One for All and All for Lunch, and published in 2009.

Michael Lawrence

Each Jiggy book is a story in its own right, but if you would like to read them in the order in which they were written, it is:

The Poltergoose, The Killer Underpants
The Toilet of Doom, Maggot Pie
The Snottle, Nudie Dudie
Neville the Devil, Ryan's Brain
The Iron, the Switch and the Broom Cupboard
Kid Swap

ONE FOR ALL AND ALL FOR LUNCH!
Visit Michael at his website: www.wordybug.com

ORCHARD BOOKS
338 Euston Road, London NW1 3BH
Orchard Books Australia
Level 17/207 Kent Street, Sydney, NSW 2000
ISBN 978 1 40830 273 6
A Paperback Original
First published in 2008 by Orchard Books
Text © Michael Lawrence 2008
Illustrations © Ellis Nadler 2008
The rights of Michael Lawrence to be identified as the
author and of Ellis Nadler to be identified as the illustrator of this
work have been asserted by them in accordance with the
Copyrights, Designs and Patents Act, 1988.
A CIP catalogue record for this book is available from the British Library
3 5 7 9 10 8 6 4 2
Printed and bound by CPI Cox & Wyman, Reading, RG1 8EX

Orchard Books is a division of Hachette Children's Books,
an Hachette Livre UK company.
www.hachettelivre.co.uk

A JIGGY McCUE STORY

Michael Lawrence

ORCHARD BOOKS

To Jiggy and Co's many fans!

Chapter one

Have you ever wished you lived under a different roof? I mean in a different house, flat, basement, with different people, wallpaper, toilets? Course you have. Who hasn't? But I bet you've never been traded for another kid, have you? Well, guess who has. Yes, the one and only Jiggy McCue. And by my own *parents* would you believe!

The first I heard about it was one Wednesday, towards the end of my mother's idea of an evening meal – the latest vegetable dish she'd failed to learn how to make from a celebrity chef with a stupid haircut.

'Jiggy,' said Mum.

'Mother,' I replied, pressing the pain in my chest.

'We have something to tell you,' she said.

'Text me,' I said. 'I'm going to my room to lie down.'

'You'll stay right there while I talk to you,' said she.

'I'll leave it to you, Peg,' said Dad, getting up.

'Oh no you won't,' said Mum. 'Sit down.'

Dad sank back in his chair. This was starting to sound serious.

'What's going on?' I asked, trying not to seem nervous.

Mum took a deep breath, which made me even more nervous. Deep breaths before speaking in my house mean Heavy Subjects are about to zoom Jigward. Had I been expelled from school while I was filing my nails? Was my pathetic chocolate ration going to be reduced to zero? Was Mum leaving Dad for a man?

But even though it was my mother's deep breath, it was my father who got in first with the news. The first bit of it anyway.

'Jig,' he said. 'We're going to swap you for another kid.'

I gawped at him. He was joking, of course.

'You're joking, of course.'

He smiled. 'Nope. Perfectly serious.'

'You're going to swap me for another kid?' I said.

'Another boy.' This was Mum. She was smiling too now.

'You're going to swap me for another *boy*?'

'It was your mother's idea,' Dad said, trying to shift the blame and failing.

I gawped some more, at both of them. What kind of parents would swap their own son?

'What kind of parents would swap their own son?' I asked.

'The kind that need the money,' said Mum. 'As you know, we had to cancel the week's touring holiday we were so looking forward to.'

'Whoa,' I said. 'Back a bit. You're swapping me for *money*?'

'Well, you don't think we'd just *give* you away, do you?' said Dad.

'Your dad's out of work,' Mum said.

'So what's new?' I said.

'So I can't pay the mortgage on my wages alone. And I'll be off work myself in a couple of months too, so no more overtime for a while. In other words, there's going to be a bit of a cash-flow problem.'

The Dad/work thing was true enough. He'd lost his job a few weeks earlier. He's always losing something, my dad. Keys, temper, hair. But his job. So selfish. Thanks to him we'd already had to cut back on essentials like my favourite biscuits, fizzy drinks, the tasty little packet snacks that Mum keeps threatening to ban. There was even talk of 'looking at my pocket money', which you could already count on the fingers of half a hand.

'Dad could get another job,' I said.

'He *could*,' said Mum. 'But you're talking about someone who's proud to wear a T-shirt with "WORK-SHY" in big EasyJet letters across the chest.'

'All right, that's him. But why will you be off work?'

'Why? I'm expecting a baby. Your little sister. Had you forgotten?'

I glanced at her stomach, which was almost as big as the downstairs cloakroom. No chance of forgetting that. 'But you've got two months yet. And what's the big deal anyway? You go to the hospital one afternoon, have her and a cup of tea, back at work next morning. Dad and I can look after her.'

Mum sighed. 'Jiggy, you're being swapped, and that's that. You should look upon it as an experience. Most kids would jump at it.'

'You *think*?'

'I do. It's quite a privilege to be selected.

You wouldn't believe the number of applicants.'

'Applicants? You actually *applied* to swap me?'

'It's the way it works, Jig,' my treacherous father explained.

'I don't believe you can make money by swapping kids,' I said feebly. 'I just do *not* believe it.'

'Oh, but you can,' Mum said brightly. 'And by doing so we'll be able to pay the mortgage for six whole months.'

'*And* have enough over for a long weekend on a canal,' said Dad.

'But me!' I cried. 'Your number one son! Your only child so far!'

Mum looked at Dad. Dad looked at Mum.

'Maybe he should hear the details,' she said to him.

'I thought he was hearing them,' said he to her.

'I don't *want* the details!' I yelled, and ran out, slammed the door, pounded up to my room, slammed that door too, and punched Roger, my toy monkey.

They gave it thirty-two minutes before coming up to see if I'd got used to the idea yet. Those thirty-two minutes included twenty-five for Mum to watch *Home and Away*. *Home and Away*. Said it all, didn't it? They were staying home and sending me away.

They knocked on my door. Well, one of them did. Dad, I guessed. My mother hardly ever knocks. She barges in, all hours, day or night, usually screeching at me to change my underwear, get a move on, or do stuff I've been trying not to think about, like homework. The knock meant that part two of Sell Your Son to the Nearest Bidder was about to occur.

'Jiggy, we have to explain,' Mum said, flinging the door back when the knock was answered with a leave-me-in-peace-forever-you-pathetic-excuse-for-parents silence. Dad shuffled in after her, looking a bit guilty. So he should.

'There's nothing *to* explain,' I snarled. 'You want to get rid of me, end of saga.'

'It's not that,' she said, plonking herself on the bed beside me and squeezing my shoulder. 'It's not that at *all*, darling.'

'Don't darling me,' I snapped, shrugging her off. 'You don't want me any more and that's that. Probably never did. It's because I can't keep still, isn't it?'

'Oh, Jiggy.'

'And don't "Oh, Jiggy" me either.'

'Calm down, Jig,' Dad said from the door. (He looked like he wanted to make a bolt for it.*) 'We have to talk this through.'

'Talk it through with me?' I said. 'Why? I'm just some unwanted kid who happens to be related to you by a freak of nature.'

He ignored this, probably because it was true. 'It'll be a real experience for you,' he said. 'Chance to see how the other half lives.'

'Other half?'

'The rich half.'

'They're rich?' I said.

'That's the impression we get.'

'Oh, so *they're* paying you. Have they got a son they don't like either then?'

'No, no, the money's not coming from them,' said Mum.

'Who then? The government? Is this some new government initiative to place kids with more loving families?'

'The television company's paying for it.'

'The what?'

'The TV company that's going to film it all.'

'Film what all?'

---

* Which would have been nice. I wasn't allowed a bolt on my door.

'If you'll just sit quiet a moment, we'll tell you,' Dad said.

So I sat quiet. Wasn't easy to keep still, though. My elbows flapped like they were battery-operated and my feet Riverdanced like maniacs. (They do this when I'm upset or agitated.)

If you want to hear about the cruel deal my parents had set up for me, drag your eyes to the next page. I wouldn't bother personally, but it's your time you're wasting, not mine.

Chapter Two

Did you ever see any of those TV programmes where people are swapped to see how they get on with different people or in different situations? Two families switch holidays or homes or wives for a while, and there are all these rows and lots of sulking and talking about one another behind their backs. Well, a new series was being made, and this was what my parents had signed us up for. It was going to be called Kid Swap. In Kid Swap, two families would exchange one child of about the same age, and cameras would go into each home and record everything.

When I heard that I was going to be in this thing like it or not, which I didn't, I shook my head in a neat combination of horror and amazement. 'Have you seen what *happens* on those shows?' I said.

'What do you mean?' This was Mum.

'People break down. Have tantrums. Throw things. They whisper to camera by torchlight and have to swear sixteen times in every sentence.'

'I can do that,' said Dad.

'That sort of thing happens in *other* shows,' Mum said. 'Carla, the nice girl from the television company, assured us that Kid Swap is going to be much classier.'

'And you believed her,' I said pityingly.

Dad smiled. 'She was quite a looker.'

I shook my head again, this time in sorrow. Parents. So easy to con. I should know, I con mine all the time. I explained, as gently as I could, to the feeble-minded old souls.

'Those TV types tell you what they think you want to hear to get you on board,' I said. 'It's only later, when you've invited your friends and relatives round to watch the result while nibbling cheese straws that you realise what a fool you've been made to look, and hear yourself say all the things they promised to leave on the cutting-room floor.'

Mum laughed. 'Jiggy, you're such a cynic. You're going to have a whale of a time. Trust me. But even if you don't, it'll all be over in a couple of weeks, then you're back home again.'

Yes, that was the one plus to all this. Two weeks of filming and that would be it. Could be a long two weeks, though.

I felt something brush my ankles. I looked down. Stallone, our cat, had crept upstairs and joined us. But he wasn't brushing my ankles out of affection. Stallone doesn't do affection. He was doing it because he'd just been outside rolling in something disgusting and wanted to pass it on. He looked up at me and snarled, the way he does.

'Here's a thought,' I said to my unfaithful parents. 'Tell the company you've change your minds about Kid Swap and'll wait for Pet Swap. Then we can exchange Stallone and see how we adapt to a terrapin or something.'

'No can do,' Dad said. 'The contract's been signed. And you want to count yourself lucky it's not Gender Swap (though they'd probably call it Sex Swap to get more viewers). If it was Gender Swap or Sex Swap, you'd have to become a girl.'

I'd already been there and done that, but that's between me and you.* 'What I want to know,' I said, 'is why I'm the last to hear about this, seeing as I'm the victim.'

'We thought we should keep quiet about it till we knew we'd been selected,' Mum said. 'Wanted it to be a surprise.'

I glared at her. 'Oh, it's that all right.'

---

* See the third Jiggy book, *The Toilet of Doom*.

'I didn't know about it either till she told me we had to go and meet the producers,' my father added, polishing his e-Bay halo.

I swivelled the glare his way. 'Went along with it then though, didn't you?'

He shrugged. 'Be a crime to turn down the loot they're offering.'

'Anyway, it was all kind of rushed,' Mum said. 'Four of the six episodes have already been filmed apparently, and the fifth is underway. I applied months ago and didn't hear a thing, but one of the families who'd agreed to do the sixth episode pulled out at the last minute, so they had to find a replacement family.'

'And there we were,' I said, 'just waiting for them like three sitting ducks. What's my share?'

'Your share?'

'What do I get out of this lousy deal?'

'You continue to have a roof over your head when you're back in the family fold,' said Dad.

'Oh joy. How come the producers didn't want to meet me too?'

'They did,' said Mum. 'We told them you weren't well.'

'Showed them some video I took one of the many

times you were in a stinking mood and not talking to anyone,' Dad said.

'Thought you'd show them my best side, did you?'

'You know how these shows work, Jig. It's not good telly if everyone's all sunny and cuddly. Thought we stood more of a chance of getting picked if our son came across as a surly little git.'

'Did the trick too,' said Mum brightly.

'And there's going to be a party at the end of shooting,' said Dad.

'I hate parties,' I muttered.

'A fancy dress party,' said Mum.

'Those most of all.'

Then they told me what they knew about the family they were farming me out to. It wasn't much. But guess what they were called, this family. Next. Yes, fans, I was being handed over to the Next Family! Mr Next's first name was Solomon, Mrs Next's was Roo (what kind of name is *that*?), and their two kids were Toby and Jess. Toby was the 13-year-old boy who was going to take my place on the McCue toilet, and Jess was the 15-year-old girl I would have to put up with as a temp sister. I asked where these people lived. Not that I cared.

'Just the other side of town,' said Mum.

'The fat cat side,' Dad smirked.

'Fat cat' must have offended Stallone, because he stalked out of the room with his tail in the air. It wasn't a view I needed right now.

'The telly people said they try to get families who live quite near one another so the crew can get from one to the other with ease,' Mum said.

'Have you met them?'

'We'll meet for the first time on Saturday. Then you'll go with them and Toby will come home with us.'

'Saturday? This Saturday?'

'Yes.'

'But that's the first day of the summer hols! I won't have any time to unwind from this long miserable term at school!'

This was all happening too fast, but it looked like it was going ahead whatever I said or wanted. I tried to find a bright side.

'How rich is this family?'

'Well, Carla said they have horses and a swimming pool,' Mum said.

'Indoor pool,' said Dad. 'Heated.'

'I've never ridden a horse, and I'm not huge on swimming.'

'I shouldn't think they're obligatory activities.'
Mum again. 'Unless they insist.'

'Insist? You mean they can make me?'

'Well, you might not *have* to do things their way,
but if you don't...'

'If I don't?'

Dad stepped in. 'If you don't, the sneery voice-
over merchant could make you look like a sulky
brat. These shows love a grouch.'

'I thought you said Kid Swap wouldn't be like the
others,' I said.

He leered. 'That was your mother.'

Chapter Three

The Saturday afternoon of Day One of my foiled summer break was warm. To celebrate the warmth, a mammoth swarm of flies had turned out to bug us as we gathered in the Councillor Snit Memorial Park, where the meeting with the Next Family was to take place. The meet actually occurred in the park café that wasn't usually open because they can't find any immigrants to work for slave-wages. The café was not only open today but pretty crowded. It was quite dark in there, mainly because the windows were small and only one light bulb seemed to be working, but a telly person managed to pick Mum and Dad out and lead them away. No one bothered to lead me, so I loitered in the shadows hoping everyone would forget I was supposed to be part of this. But then I heard a voice across the room say 'Where's Jimmy?' and Mum say 'It's Jiggy.'

'What is?' asked the person who'd wondered about Jimmy.

'His name.'

'Jiggy? I thought it was Jimmy. It's Jimmy on the contract.'

'Well, it shouldn't be. He's called Jiggy.'

'OK, but where is he?'

Mum called me over and introduced me to the geezer who thought my name was Jimmy. This turned out to be the director, who called himself DD, which might have been short for Donald Duck for all I knew. I'd met DD outside. Seen him anyway. He was a real charm-artist, a real smoothy. Quite tall, fake tan, fair hair that flopped over one eye, mouth stacked with teeth so perfect they had to have been filed down and painted with Dazzle White Silk from SmartSave. And he had this voice that kind of oozed over you like it had been oiled or something. I glanced at Dad. We swapped sour expressions. I glanced at Mum. She didn't look sour. Her eyes were brighter than the café light bulb as they clocked DD. I knew that look. She thought he was really something. So did Dad and I, but a different something.

When DD said, 'Jimmy, come and meet the Next Family,' my mother didn't bother to correct him a second time. She pushed me forward and stood behind me, hands on my shoulders like I was a sack of old clothes she was giving to Oxfam. I peered through the non-light at these four people, who peered back. While DD was introducing me to them (as 'Jimmy') and them to me, someone flicked a switch and an ocean of light zipped the room apart. All us non-telly folk staggered with our arms over our eyes as the switch-flicker yelled, 'Sorry, shoulda warned ya!' and we tried to make sense of this bright new world through the blue circles leap-frogging across our eyeballs.

I still couldn't see properly when the director with the initials of a cartoon duck told us to get ready for the first scene, which was going to be the two families pretending we hadn't already met. Then the camera was rolling, or rocking, or whatever it is cameras do, and DD yelled 'QUIET!', and Mum and Dad and Mr and Mrs Next were shaking hands – and whispering.

DD stopped the camera. 'When I say "Quiet",' he said to the two prongs of parents, 'I mean everyone but you. What I would like you to do is say something like, "Hi, how are you", and "Pleased to meet you, this is Blah, and Blah, and my name's Blah." OK?'

I just wished that when he told the cameraman to 'Go again, Jack,' the parents had said exactly that – Blah, Blah and Blah – but they gave their proper names (I immediately forgot the other family's, like I had when Mum told me them the first time) so I continued not to chuckle about being there. When this scene was done we were all sat down at the tables that were never used, and told to talk about ourselves, also for the camera. I wanted to sink into my shirt when my mother got going. Half of what she said was total fantasy in a trying-too-hard voice, and the rest, when she relaxed a bit, was about what morons me and Dad are. Dad tried to shove an oar in every now and then to row her back to reality, but she silenced him with an arm grip, and once by slapping a palm over his teeth. It was like she'd been waiting for a chance to diss us to the world for years. I just sat there, head down, trying to beam myself to Jupiter. The whole town was going to hear these lies about me and my family! The whole country!

There were a few retakes when Mum or Mrs and Mr Next (Mrs had this mass of flying orange hair) said something the director thought could be improved, or a helicopter looking for escaped convicts flew over, but this toe-curling scene was wrapped up inside forty or fifty minutes. Then everyone hung about outside the café that rarely opened, where the flies of the world had come to hover and zzzz. Did I mention the flies? I'd never seen so many in one go. One summer there'd been a plague of ladybirds. Another, there'd been a deluge of those tiny black midges that get into all your nooks and grannies. This year it was the turn of the flies. While I stood waving my arms and failing to massacre them, everyone chatted and chuckled like there were no flies at all and they'd known one another for yonkos – specially Mum, whose voice seemed to be stuck on 'loud' now that she knew she was going to be one of the no-talent celebs that everyone but me seems to want to be. I almost ran out of the park with my head in my arms when she told Mrs Next that she spent a fortune every summer trying to 'factor my skin to a colour just *half* your shade!' Mrs N grinned and said, 'Mine was factored in at birth,' and Mr Next said his was too, and that having Polynesian parents helped. Dad whispered to me that they were a 'good-looking family,' but I knew that he was thinking of Mrs Next more than the male Nexts.

I kept well out of all this. Only spoke when spoken to, and even then kept the word count as close to zero as humanly possible. When the Next daughter came up and tried to talk, I told her to save it for the cameras.

'Oh, you're going to be a lot of fun,' she said.

'Don't bet on it,' I said.

I didn't speak at all to the brother who was going to move into my house. He was grinning his head off at everyone, which made them grin back at him. No chance of getting a grinfest going with me. When he flashed his pearlies my way, I turned to face some bushes.

'Hey, Jig.'

This came from the bushes.

'Pete?' I said.

'And Angie,' the bushes answered.

I glanced over my shoulder. No one seemed to be watching. I plunged into the bushes.

'My foot!' Angie said.

'Your fault for leaving it there,' I said, pulling leaves across so they covered me too.

Naturally, I'd told Pete and Angie about Kid Swap, and naturally Pete had laughed his stupid socks off. Angie had been more sympathetic, specially when

31

she heard that the Next Family had horses.

'I always wanted to ride,' she'd said kind of dreamily.

'You can,' I'd replied. 'Stick a carrot down your jeans and pretend you're me. I'll live at your house for two weeks and wear eye-liner.'

'I don't wear eye-liner.'

'You should. Do wonders for you.'

But that was the other day. Today she asked how it was going so far. I told her that it wasn't. She said I was a misery. 'Most people would trade their Xboxes for a chance to appear on telly,' she said.

'I haven't got an Xbox.'

'Well, if nothing else, look on it as a break from your folks. You never stop moaning about them, after all.'

'Moaning about them is what parents are there for,' I said. 'If they weren't there I'd be stuck for moan material.'

'Oh, not you,' she said. 'Not for long.'

'These flies!' said Pete, batting away a bunch that had lurched with me into the bushes.

'What's the other boy like?' Angie asked.

'What other boy?'

'The one who's taking your place at McCue Mansions.'

'Dunno. Haven't spoken. He seems to have some sort of mouth deformity.'

'It's called a smile, Jig.'

'You call it a smile if you want. Smarm like that doesn't work on me.'

'I wonder why flies are called flies?' Pete said.

Angie and I looked at him amid the leaves. 'What?' we said.

'I was wondering why flies are called flies.'

'Because they fly,' Angie said. 'Why else?'

'So do birds,' said Pete.

'I don't get you.'

'I mean birds fly too, but we don't call *them* flies.'

'You couldn't call birds flies,' I said. 'If you called birds flies as well as flies you wouldn't be able to tell one from the other.'

'You would if you looked.'

'But not if you were just talking about them.'

'Why would I talk about them?'

'You tell me, you brought them up.'

'I didn't bring them up. I just said, "Why are flies called flies?" And I'll say it again. Why are flies called flies? If you called everything by what they

33

do, tortoises would be called slow, cats would be called meows, and dogs would be called crap.'

'Mantelpieces would still be called mantelpieces,' said Angie. 'So would chairs.'

'Mantelpieces and chairs don't do anything,' Pete said. 'Neither do tables. They just are, so they keep their names. Flies are different. They move.'

He tried to squash a couple between his hands to prove it. Missed.

'Flies aren't *only* called flies,' Angie said.

'Uh?' said Pete.

'They're also called house-flies. When you say "house-fly", you know exactly what kind of creature you're talking about.'

'You might if they stayed in the house,' I said, swiping at a few. 'This lot are nowhere near a house. You can't suddenly call them park-flies just because they've nipped out for a sec.'

'And what about the ones at the council tip?' said Pete. 'Get herds of flies there. You don't call them council-tip-flies.'

'Swarms,' said Angie.

'What?'

'Bundles of flies come in swarms, not herds.'

'Isn't that bees?' I said.

'If it's bees, what are herds of flies called?' Angie wanted to know.

We weren't sure.

'I know what a swarm of kangaroos is,' said Pete.

'What?' I asked.

'A mob.'

'A mob?'

'Yeah.'

'A mob of kangaroos?'

'Yeah.'

'Everyone knows that,' Angie said.

'I don't,' I said.

'Everyone but you.'

'Bet Eejit Atkins doesn't.'

'I wouldn't boast about knowing as little as Atkins if I were you.'

'Roo,' I said suddenly.

'Eh?' said Pete.

'Roo. The name of the Next mother. I just remembered.'

'Next mother?' said Angie.

'My new family is called Next.'

'Get away.'

'No, really.'

'And her name's Woo?'

'Roo.'

'Does she hop?' said Pete. 'Keep babies in her pouch?'

'Dunno. Guess I'll find out over the next two weeks.'

'The "*Next* two weeks",' said Angie with a leafy smile.

'Witty,' I said, and plunged out of the bushes chewing flies.

Chapter Four

Before my parents handed me over to the Next Family, my mother did the Big Farewell scene for the camera, hugging me tight and piling on the tears like she was actually going to miss me. Ha! Fortunately, my father stood well out of range. No chance of the world seeing *him* hug his son. Fine with me.

Then me and Toby were told to do the actual swap scene, walking towards one another while the wrong parents waited for us. It felt like a hostage exchange in a film. All we needed was a long bridge and cars and men with guns and sunglasses. I didn't like the look of Toby. His hair was too long and shiny, he looked too confident, he was bigger than me, and that grin of his was still stretching his features like he was all for this TV deal. As we were about to pass he raised a hand for a high-five. I almost gave him a low-two instead, but managed to keep my hands in my pockets all the way to his parents. I hoped the camera caught my scowl. I didn't plan on making this a breeze for that flop-head director.

Then I went off with the Next Family in their car, which was parked by the park gates. It was a nice car, newish and roomy, not a manky old heap like ours. They got all talkative as we drove, but I wasn't in the mood so they dried up before we got to theirs.

The Next house was in one of those just out-of-town roads where the properties have parking space for juggernauts. It wasn't much older than my house, but it was four times the size, with grass and trees all round it instead of a little garden back and front and a broken street lamp by the gate. They didn't have an ordinary gate either. They had two really big ones, all fancy ironwork and stuff, which were already open when we got there. The TV mob had raced on ahead in their van so they could be there when we arrived and film us getting out of the car. DD, the director, didn't travel with the others. He had this flash red sports number with the lid thrown back and a personalised number plate: DD2P.

Inside the house, the cameraman filmed the Next parents and daughter but not me, which I had no complaints about. DD stood beside the camera asking them questions like, 'How do you think it's going to feel having a different boy in the family?'

The parents said they thought it would be fun. The daughter – Jess – smiled and said, 'Cool.' Then she glanced at me, and said, 'I guess.'

When she'd done her bit, Jess took me on a tour of the house. She was taller than me, and she had bosoms because she was fifteen and a girl. She seemed quite a chirpy sort, so as it was just her and me and no cameras I thought that I'd make a bit of an effort. I switched on the famous McCue charm in the hall (which was about as wide as our living room) and pointed to the portrait type paintings on the walls.

'Who are the freaks?'

Jess laughed. 'Relatives, going way back. Not the most attractive bunch, are they?'

'What's with all the tattoos, beads and wacky headgear?'

'Part of Polynesian tradition. The word "tattoo" is of Polynesian origin, in case you didn't know.'

'I didn't. Your name, Next, is that Polynesian?'

'Not exactly. But it's been the family name on my dad's side since the seventeen hundreds.'

'How come?'

'We're descended from an English pirate called Jeremy Next.'

'A pirate!'

'Also known as The Black Scab. Quite a character by all accounts. Next was probably not his real name, but he made it his own. He would attack a vessel, loot it, sink it – sometimes with everyone still on board – return to his own ship, point out to sea, and shout "Next!".'

'So how are you descended from him?'

'He finally settled in the islands, married a local woman, and their kids were called Next. Simple as that. Talking of names...'

'Yes?'

'Jiggy. I'm guessing it wasn't given to you at birth.'

I stared at her. 'You're the first to get my name right today.'

She winked. 'Maybe I'm the first to pay attention.'

I explained that I got the nickname when I was little and even more fidgety than I am now. She said 'Cool' again, then asked me what was wrong.

'Wrong?'

'You don't seem very happy to be here.'

I sighed. 'Ah, it's this Kid Swap thing.'

'Not so keen, eh?'

'I wasn't consulted. Is your brother keen?'

'Oh yes, he's really up for it. Toby likes anything new.'

'What about your mum and dad? They doing it for the moolah like mine? You wouldn't know they needed it, looking at this place.'

'They don't. They're in it for the publicity.'

'Publicity?'

'They're Sans-earthists. We all are. Ma and Pa hope our episode will tune a few viewers in to our beliefs.'

'Sans-whatists?'

'Earthists. Haven't you heard of us?'

'Don't think so. Beliefs?'

She giggled. 'You'll see.'

Now I was worried. Was I going to be at the mercy of a coven of religious nutcakes for a fortnight? Would there be kneeling at dawn? Group humming? Holding hands with our eyes shut before every meal?

* * *

On the chest of drawers in Toby's bedroom there was a framed photo of him and his family smiling arm-in-arm. Toby had the biggest smile of all.

41

Well, why wouldn't he? He had it made, in this family. There were also two greetings-type cards, standing side by side. Inside one of them his parents had written 'Good luck, Toby!' and added lots of crosses. Inside the other card were the words 'Hope it goes well, Jimmy!' It was signed 'Toby'. I tore the second card to shreds and stuffed the shreds in the bottom of the suitcase I'd brought with me. I left the other card on the chest-of-drawers, but face down, like it had fallen over. I would have shoved the photo in one of the drawers, but someone might come in and wonder where it was, so I just nudged it so it faced away from where I would see it most of the time. That way it looked like it had been knocked by accident.

Toby's room was twice the size of mine at home, and it had all the mod cons, like a games console, a TV that actually worked, and a double bed. He had his own en-suite bathroom too. And everything was so *tidy*. It was tidy because the Next Family had a housekeeper to clear up after them. They also had a maid, a real maid, in a real maid's uniform. The housekeeper and the maid had obviously been told my wrong name, because when I met them the housekeeper (Mrs Moult, who did the cooking too) said, 'How do you do, Master Jimmy,' and the maid said, 'I'm Betty, Master Jimmy, if you need anything just ring your bell.'

My bell? I had a *bell*? I'd noticed one set into the wall by the bed and wondered what it was for. Now I knew. I didn't put them right about my name because I was too busy chasing the words 'Holy cow' round my skull. What was it Dad said about finding out how the other half lives?

It helped that the TV crew weren't there to film me eating my first evening meal at the Next house, but it felt very strange having someone wait on me who wasn't a mother. I was worried that they would have a butler or footman as well, but Mrs Moult and Betty the maid brought the fodder in, and they were nice and relaxed about it, so I didn't mind them too much. What they served was a chunk of some bird in a creamy sauce with this curly stuff on the side. Roo asked me if it was all right. I said it was, and I didn't lie. For afters we had something thick and chocolate-coloured, except it wasn't chocolate. It was terrific, and when this was out of the way Roo asked if I'd missed the fruit and veg.

'Fruit and veg? There wasn't any − was there?'

'No, that's why I'm asking if you missed it.'

'I never miss fruit and veg. Specially veg.'

'You don't like them?'

'Doesn't matter if I do, my mother makes me eat them.'

'Well, we don't do that here.'

'Great. There's never any peace at home. "Eat the fruit," Mum says, and "Jiggy, don't you dare leave that broccoli!" I get it all the time.'

'Jiggy?' said Solomon.

'Yes?' I said.

'You said that's what your mum calls you.'

'That's right.'

'But your name's Jimmy.'

'No it's not, it's Jiggy.'

'I'm sure I heard that director chap call you Jimmy.'

'You did,' said Jess, my borrowed sister. 'That man's a plank.'

'A plank,' said Solomon. 'And that is ... what exactly?'

'Long flat bit of wood,' I explained.

'And in human terms?'

'Long flat bit of flesh, bone and smarm.'

'Doesn't sound as if you've become all that attached to DD,' he said.

'PP,' I said. 'And you're right, I haven't.'

'PP?'

'If he can't get my name right, he can whistle for his initials.'

Solomon laughed. So did Roo and Jess. I asked them when the TV crew were coming back.

'First thing in the morning,' said Roo. 'DD said he wants to film us going about our day. We're to act as though they're not here.'

'No problem for me,' I said. 'I'll wear a blindfold and shove bubble gum in my ears.'

They laughed at this too. I looked round at those three jolly faces and felt kind of warm inside. Hey, I thought, maybe this isn't gonna be such a rough ride after all.

I might have added something else to that. Something like, Hey-double-hey, I'm Jiggy McCue, who kiddeth I? Since when did rides not get rough for me?

But I didn't. I never learn.

Chapter Five

Morning. Woke up, cranked the old lids back a frac, didn't recognise the ceiling, or the wall when I turned my head to the left, and for a panicky mo thought I was back at the Boy Factory. Did I ever tell you about the Boy Factory? Well, when I was young, whenever I annoyed my father he would say, 'Jig, if you don't behave, it's back to the Boy Factory for you.' He'd brought me up to believe that boys were sent back where they came from for recycling if they played up. I was terrified of being sent back to the factory, and became as good as gold every time. Did the trick for years till I finally cottoned on. And here I was, age thirteen, waking up thinking my parents had finally carried out their threat.

But like I said, it was only for a mo. Then I remembered where I really was and closed my eyes again, stretched my legs and arms as far as they would go. My stretched fingers reached the headboard and climbed the wall, where they brushed a poster of a cabbage with a big red cross on it. Just as I fingertipped the crossed cabbage a voice that wasn't in a distant galaxy, said 'That's it, hold that stretch now, Jimmy,' and I twisted sharply to my right, flipped out of bed, and thudded onto the rug with my btm stoking the airways.

'Wha?' I said, like you do at such times. Then I said, 'Err?', like you also do if you're me.

'Oh, the viewers are going to *love* you, Jimmy!' the voice said.

My bum and I looked towards the door. PP and his cameraman had just filmed me leaping sideways for millions of total strangers to hoot at and slap one another's back.

'Whajadoinere?' I demanded, jumping to my feet and covering my pyjama front seconds after the gusset sprang apart for the eyes of the same millions of total strangers.

'We're filming the family starting their day,' said PP.

'So go and film them!'

'We've done Solomon setting off for work and Roo saying goodbye to him, but Jess locked herself in her room and says she won't come out till she's got her face on.'

'Well the same goes for me!'

I ran into Toby's en-suite, slammed the door, and spun round to flick the key or bang the bolt. Except... no key, no bolt.* I looked for something to wedge against the door. The only thing that could be moved was the wooden towel rail but it wasn't heavy enough to keep a geriatric budgie out, let alone full-grown cameramen and directors. Nothing for it but to stand as near the toilet as I could with one leg bent right back, sole of foot on door behind me, and take aim. Then I washed my hands like I've always been ordered to at gunpoint, and brushed my teeth. Usually I brush the McCue choppers after breakfast, but I wasn't at home now and didn't know the rules here. In my usual bathroom my toothbrush is one of three standing to attention in a rack, but there wasn't even one here because in all the non-excitement I'd forgotten to brush the night before. I unzipped the fake crocodile-skin washbag Mum had bought specially and found a new brush and tube of paste inside, plus a flannel and an unwrapped bar of soap. She might as well not have bothered with the soap and flannel. The only time I use flannels is when she stands over me with her hands on her hips saying

---

* Don't you just hate it when you visit someone's bathroom and find there's no way to keep people from flinging the door back whenever they feel like it? Bathrooms should be treated as sacred places, like churches used to be before they were turned into wine shops. You go to the bathroom to be alone with whatever you have to do, not to do it while someone's mother or sister stands there taking notes.

something unfriendly like, 'Wash that filthy neck, Jiggy – now!' As for soap, there was one of those squirty dispenser things on the shelf behind the basin that I can never get to work if someone hasn't used it first.

When I'd done my teeth, I opened the door and was about to step out when I noticed the camera under my nose. I slammed the door and yelled 'Get out of here!' through it. I waited a minute before peeking out again. They'd gone. I marched to the bedroom door, kicked it shut, and wedged the room's only chair under the handle.

Getting dressed is something else I don't normally do before breakfast, but I always feel wrong in my PJs in someone else's house, specially when I have a flapping gusset and my mother forgets to pack my dressing gown, like this time. Pity there isn't a Parent Factory to return faulty Golden Oldies to, I thought as I pulled my pants on.

Even though I was dressed, I felt kind of weird going down to my first breakfast with the Next Family. It was about half eight, but I didn't know if I should've been there earlier, or what. I needn't have worried. None of the family were in the dining room, just Betty the maid, moving stuff around.

'Morning, Master Jimmy,' Betty said. 'And how are you today?'

'Terrific,' I answered. 'And it's Jiggy.'

'Jiggy? What's that?'

'My name.'

'Oh? I thought it was Jimmy.'

'No. Jiggy. Pass it along, eh? How does breakfast work here?'

'I serve you,' she said, and waved a hand at a batch of shiny silver plate covers. 'We have eggs, bacon, sausage and black pudding.'

'Any Choco Nuggets?'

'Choco Nuggets?'

'My favourite cereal.'

'Oh, you won't find any cereals here,' Betty said.

'What, none?'

'None. You must know that, Master Jimmy.'

'Jiggy.'

'Master Jiggy.'

'And whaddayasay we drop the "Master"? I'm nobody's master.'

'Oh, I can't. It's the standard mode of address for the Next son and heir.'

'I'm not the Next son and heir. I'm not even the Last one.'

'Still, I think it's expected that I address you that way.'

'Well. All right. But if there are no cereals, could I have toast please?'

Betty laughed. 'Toast! You'll be lucky.'

'Will I?'

'Bread is another absolute no-no. It's the flour.'

'The flour?'

She leant closer, and whispered, 'They're Sans-earthists.'

'So I heard,' I whispered back. 'What I haven't heard is what Sans-earthists are.'

She looked surprised. 'You don't know?'

'No, I— '

'Morning, Jiggy!'

Mrs Next – Roo – had just come in. She wore a green silk kimono and matching slippers with curly toes, and her mad orange hair stood out even more than yesterday, like she'd had a fright. (PP followed her in, so maybe she had.) Jack the cameraman came too, and his assistant, Boz, and this girl, Carla. Boz and Carla looked about seventeen.

'Hope you slept well,' Roo said.

'Could be worse, I said. 'You?'

'Oh yes, I always do. Breakfasted yet?'

'No, I was just talking about it to...'

I chinned Betty. I didn't like to say her name because I didn't know her well enough – and I couldn't say 'the maid'.

Jack the cameraman started filming us. There was a microphone attached to his camera, so I supposed he picked up our every word and sniff as well as our every twitch and scratch. Roo told Betty we would help ourselves, Betty went, and Roo lifted the covers to show me piles of bacon rashers, sausages, eggs, and lumps of black stuff that looked like dinosaur whoopsy.

'Anything you fancy?' she asked me.

'I usually just have cereal or toast,' I said.

She laughed. Hooted rather. That lady had a real laugh on her. One of those laughs where the person throws their whole mouth open and just roars for eight seconds, then stops like the plug's been pulled.

'Cereal or toast!' she said at the end of the hoot. 'Didn't anyone tell you that we're Sans-earthists?'

'They told me, but they didn't say what it means.'

She started loading food onto a pair of plates. 'It means that we don't eat anything that issues from the ground.'

'The ground? You mean like...'

'Fruit and vegetables.'

'Ohhhh, I see. So you only eat flesh?'

'Oh, no, not *just* flesh. Also processed foods that don't use plant extracts. Selected sweets and carbonated drinks are fine too.'

Sweets and fizzy. Things were looking up. And no fruit and veg. *Way* up.

Roo must have seen the light go on in my eyes, because she smiled and said, 'We get by.'

She handed me one of the loaded plates and we sat down at the long dining table. Jack's camera stayed on us, but I had no trouble ignoring it with extinct dino whoopsy in front of me.

'What is this?' I asked, not quite touching it with my fork.

'Black pudding. Surely you've seen it before.'

'Probably not this close up. What's it made of?'

'Blood.'

'Blood?'

'Congealed pigs' blood.'

I gulped. 'Pigs' blood?'

'Mm, it's delicious. Give it a try.'

'Eat something made of solid blood?' I said. 'You're talking to someone who won't even suck a paper-cut on his finger.'

'That's different. That's your own. And this has been boiled.'

'Boiled blood gone hard. Hmm, tempting. Some other time maybe.'

'You don't know what you're missing,' she said, and took a big bite of Pigosaurus dropping.

I covered the black pud with a rasher, but knowing it was under it put me off the bacon and sausages, which is a shame because I quite like bacon and sausage as a rule. Roo didn't seem bothered that I only ate the eggs, but PP must have seen his chance for something he could use because he whispered to Jack and Jack nodded and zoomed his camera in on my plate. I could hear it already, the chuckling commentary that would be added to the finished film.

'Oh dear, young Jimmy seems to be a bit off his food this morning!'

Chapter Six

After my eggy brekkers I went back upstairs and put the chair against the door again. Then I dug out my mobile and speed-dialled Angie who'd told me to keep her updated on what happened here. I couldn't get a connection. Later I found out why. The TV company had set up some sort of blocking device to stop me contacting the outside world. They wanted to see how I would get on without access to my friends. Contact with my parents was also forbidden, but I probably wouldn't have bothered with them. Parents have their place, but when you get the chance to be shot of them for a pair of weeks you don't want them in your ear day and night, do you?

There was a knock on the door.

'Jimmy?' A female voice I didn't recognise.

'No one here of that name,' I said to the door.

'Jimmy, you're wanted downstairs.'

'Who by?'

'DD. He needs you for more filming.'

'Who are you?' I asked the door.

'Carla. DD's assistant.'

'Tell him I'm not well.'

'Oh, aren't you?' She sounded like she actually cared. But then she said: 'Could you come down anyway? If you're not feeling so good he'll want to get it on film. Maybe you could lie on the couch and groan a little.'

'I really don't want to do that,' I said.

'Jimmy…'

'Jiggy.'

'What?'

'My name.'

'Oh. Jimmy, please help me out here. It's my job to do what DD says, and he's told me to get you downstairs. If I don't … well, getting fired from my first proper job will look bad on my CV.'

I sighed – why am I so soft-hearted? – and took the chair from under the handle and opened the door. And there she stood. Well of course she did, but it suddenly hit me that up close she wasn't bad-looking. No, that's not right. She was utterly gorgeous. Funny I'd missed it before. She had these big green eyes and this mass of curly brown hair and when she smiled this big wide toothy smile something happened in my chest. I thought I was going to have a heart attack for a sec, but once I'd taken three or four giant breaths I got a hold of the situation. Sort of. What is it about some girls? How do they do that? No wonder so many of them were burnt as witches.

'Thanks, Jimmy,' Carla said.

This time I didn't correct her. I couldn't. My voice had packed its bags and gone to Timbuktu to sell time-shares. Carla reached for one of my arms. The left one, I think. I let her take it. She linked it with one of hers (probably the right one) and I went tingly all over and let her walk me along the landing and down the stairs.

'Jimmy!'

This was PP as Carla dragged my arm into the living room. When she let go of me, I tried to pay attention as he told me what he wanted me to do for the camera. Then we were shooting the scene and I did it without argument because most of the McCue vocal chords were still in Timbuktu. Fortunately I didn't have to speak. As we were finishing, I noticed Carla slip out of the room, and missed her right away.

'Pretty lifeless performance there, Jim,' PP said.

'Huh?'

'Looked like you were in a trance. Care to do it again?'

'No,' I said, and walked out, hoping to see Carla again.

I couldn't find her, but a bit later I saw her climb into PP's flashy car with him. Just before they went I heard PP tell Roo that they were going to Brook Farm to shoot Toby and my family. There was already another crew over there, he said, but he needed to 'input some structure there too'. Jack the cameraman and Boz his assistant stayed to 'get some exterior material'. Prat, I thought. They joined Roo and Jess and me in the kitchen for lunch, but they brought their own. Fish and chips from somewhere. Jack and Boz never said much – I don't think I ever heard anything but a grunt from Boz – but they didn't need to say anything as they unpeeled those wrappers and got stuck in while my lips licked themselves senseless with envy. As an adopted Sans-earther I couldn't have had chips because they come from potatoes, but I could have had the fish with the batter removed. Could have, if it had been offered, but what's the point of batterless battered fish? Actually, I couldn't even have had that. Betty the maid brought Roo and Jess and me something very different to fish and chips. A small bowl of pills each. There were five pills of different colours.

'We have them every lunchtime,' Roo explained. 'They're packed with nutrients and they leave you feeling full. But you do need that as well.'

'That' was a tiny cup of blue liquid that came with the pills.

'What is it?'

'A laxative.'

'A laxative?'

'Without it, with our diet, your insides will soon be like solid rock.'

I heard splutters from Jack and Boz as they crammed their faces with fish and chips. I would have spluttered too if I heard someone else told what Roo had just told me.

After 'lunch' Jess suggested that we go see the horses, and although I'm not big on seeing horses I had nothing better to do, so I said OK and she went up to her room. When she came down she wore tight horse-coloured trousers with patches on the inside leg. She also wore a hard hat with a chin strap.

On the way to the paddock we passed a big heap of manure that the Next horses had produced between them. From the way it steamed I guessed that they'd also been given the blue laxative – a bucketful each.

One of the horses was standing in the middle of the paddock gazing at nothing, like it was thinking, 'So I'm a horse. Do I really have to just *stand* here all day?' The other horse was nuzzling the fence. This one was wearing a saddle, the other one wasn't.

'Hi, horse,' I said to the fencer. It didn't answer, just blinked at me.

'Fancy a ride?' Jess asked.

She wasn't talking to the horse, so I said, 'Pardon me?'

'She's all saddled up.'

'Oh, so he's a she.'

'Yes. Well?'

'Well what?'

'Would you like to try her out?'

'No, not really.'

She unbuckled her hat and offered it to me. 'Go on.'

'I don't think so,' I said, sticking my hands behind my back.

'Don't worry,' she said, 'Genevieve's a real softy,' and jammed the helmet on my head before I could turn and run.

'No, look, I've never been on a horse.'

'She's a mare. And here's your chance.'

She buckled the strap under my chinny-chin-chin.

'I feel stupid,' I said when the hat was strapped on.

'Well, you'd better not act it.'

She nodded to her left. PP had returned, and he'd followed us, with Jack the cameraman. Jack's camera was on us.

'Oh, great,' I said.

'Come on,' Jess said, climbing up the fence.

In that hat, with that camera aimed at me, I had no choice.

Inside the paddock, Jess held her hand out to Genevieve the saddled mare and patted her neck and whispered something in one of her ears. Genevieve looked at me like she'd just been told that I was new at this and that it was fine if she wanted to trample me to death.

'Put your foot in the stirrup,' Jess said.

I looked at the stirrup. It was further off the ground than my foot usually likes to lift.

'I'm really not sure about this,' I said.

'Go on, put it in.'

I raised my foot halfway to the clouds and wiggled it into the stirrup.

'Now grip the reins and haul yourself up into the saddle.'

I gripped the reins and tried to do that small thing. The leg that wasn't attached to the foot in the stirrup lifted a little way off the ground and fell back again.

'It's a long way up there,' I said to Jess.

'I'll give you a hand,' she said.

The hand was under my left bum cheek before I knew it, and it was this – the uninvited palm of a strange girl rather than its push – that shot me up into the saddle. (I almost went right over the top and down the other side actually, but just about managed not to.)

'Keep a good hold of the reins,' Jess said when I was up there.

'I am!' I wailed.

'But not too tight. And keep your knees in.'

I tried to do those things too as she started to lead Genevieve round the paddock.

'I don't feel safe!' I moaned, crouching low.

'Give it time,' she said.

'*I don't want to give it time!*'

I didn't mean to shout, but I must have because Genevieve gave a little jump and threw her neck back. As my lips flattened against her hairy mane she broke free, and then Jess was somewhere behind us, bawling things I didn't catch because all my concentration was focused on gripping the reins. I also tried to keep my knees in like I'd been told, but it wasn't easy because my rear kept slamming down every time the saddle went up, and that saddle was not soft.

'Stop!' I screamed at Genevieve. 'Stop!'

She ignored me. Maybe she doesn't understand English, I thought as she picked up speed. I closed my eyes as we approached the fence. Kept them closed as Genevieve's hooves left the ground. Then we were sailing through the air. But not for long. In no time at all there was a jolt (front hooves landing), followed by another jolt (back hooves), and we were moving across the ground again.

I squeezed my eyes open a tad. Genevieve was galloping. Everything but the back of her neck was a blur.

She went right on galloping for about eight seconds (this is a guess, I didn't time her) before one of her hooves struck a stone and she stumbled. When she stumbled, her big fat back end lifted so suddenly that my hands were forced to let go of the reins and point at the sky. On my way to the clouds I passed several birds that seemed to find the whole thing highly amusing, but I didn't stop to tell them off because by the time I'd got the words right in my head I was zooming earthward.

Now the ground being what it is – quite hard, usually – I might have expected to have become a rather flat version of my former self on hitting it. But fortunately there was something soft waiting for me down there. Just before I reached it I noticed that Jack's camera was closely following my journey. It followed me all the way down, and was still following me as I slapped face-first, arms and legs outstretched, into the enormous heap of steaming horse manure that I'd steered so well clear of on the way to the paddock.

Chapter Seven

My mother would have fainted with shock to hear that I power-showered three times after the plunge into the manure. The reason for three showers was that after the first there were still bits of the stuff in my ears, nose and hair, and after the second I thought I still smelt a bit.

When I finally went downstairs, cleaner than I'd been since birth, Jess said she felt bad about what had happened.

'I don't feel terrifically great about it myself,' I said.

'I'll make it up to you,' she said. 'You can choose a rabbit.'

'Choose a rabbit? You have rabbits?'

'Yes, a new batch arrived the day before yesterday.'

Now I'm not really a pet person, but I like rabbits. I might have had one already, but my mother says rabbits need looking after and I wouldn't bother once the novelty wore off. Time and time again I've said that I would bother, but she won't have it.

If I took a rabbit home after my stay with the Next Family what could she do? She'd have to buy a cage, or Dad would have to make one. If Dad made one, the rabbit would be in someone else's garden by the following breakfast, but it would be a start.

Jess took me round the back of the house to this big cage full of young rabbits. I counted them. There were twelve.

'Which one do you fancy?' Jess asked.

I scanned the rabbits. They were all so cute, but there was one that caught my eye in particular. It had slightly longer fur than the rest, and it was a sort of rust-colour, and it kept looking at me like it was thinking, 'Hey, Jig, take me, take me!'

'That one,' I said.

'The orangey one?'

'Yeah. That OK?'

'It's fine. He's yours.'

'How do you know he's a he?'

'Experience.'

I leaned closer to the cage. The rusty rabbit didn't move, but he locked eyes with me, like he knew we would be together from now on.

'Come to Jig, bunny,' I said. And he came closer. 'He's smart,' I said to Jess. 'What shall I call him?'

'Oh, you don't want to give him a name,' said Jess.

'Course I do. Why wouldn't I? Don't you name your rabbits?'

'The nearest I get to naming them is giving them numbers. Numbering works.'

'Well I'm going to give mine a name,' I said. 'I'm going to call him Hector.' Don't ask me where 'Hector' came from, but it seemed to fit somehow. 'Come to Jig, Hector.'

And Hector came. I squatted down and we sat facing one another through the wire, nose to nose. He was beautiful. And so friendly. I asked Jess if I could hold him. She asked why I'd want to do that.

'Well, if he's mine...' I said.

'I don't think it's a good idea to get too attached,' she said.

'It's all right for you,' I said. 'I've never had a rabbit.'

'What, never?'

'No. Mum doesn't like them.'

'Well, no accounting for taste.'

She opened the cage, reached in, grabbed Hector – he didn't try to get away – closed the cage, handed him to me. I cradled him in my arms. He was so soft and warm. And the way he snuggled into me!

'Want to try the pool?' Jess said while I was stroking Hector.

'The pool?'

'Take a swim.'

'Oh, I'm not much of a swimmer,' I admitted.

'So just splash about. The water's lovely. We keep the temperature way up.'

I would rather have stayed there stroking my new pet, but I felt like I had to go with Jess. I kissed Hector's super-soft head and put him back in the cage. 'Bye, Hect,' I said, giving him a little wave. He looked kind of sad that I was going.

We went to the pool, which was in its own building attached to the house. Most of the roof was made of glass panels, so the sun could brighten and warm everything up. It wasn't a huge pool – about as long as most public pool widths, and the width was about half that – but it was big enough for me. There were blue-green tiles on the bottom and along the sides, and at one end there were buttons you could press if you wanted waves, and all round the edge there were these big pot-plants, and seats if you wanted to just sit.

'Cool pool,' I said to Jess.

'It'll do,' she said. 'These are the changing cubicles.'

'I've got nothing to change into.'

She pushed the door of one of the two cubicles. 'You'll find a pair of Toby's swimming trunks in that locker.'

I felt my face screw up at the thought of wearing a tog that had been glued to someone else's privates. Jess noticed.

'Don't worry, they'll have been washed since he last used them. Probably.'

I went into the cubicle and opened the little locker. Yes, there was a pair of trunks in there. Blue ones with green zigzags. Jess went into the cubicle next door and I closed the door of mine. I sniffed the trunks. They smelt clean enough.

'I'm really not a great swimmer!' I yelled through the wall as I got undressed.

'So you said,' Jess yelled back.

'Well, I'm saying it again, so you don't laugh when I splash more than normal!'

'Stop worrying. What's the worst that can happen?'

'You mean after I drown or before?' She laughed.

I stepped into the trunks that weren't mine. 'Holy swimming sacks,' I said.

'What now?' Jess asked.

'These are elephant trunks.'

'Uh?'

'Look like a free gift from Planet Huge. They're enormous!'

'Oh, come on. Toby's only a bit bigger than you.'

'That's what I thought. But you could fit three of me in these and still have room for an extra buttock.' I wasn't exaggerating. I had to hold a big fistful of the material at the front to stop the things exchanging gossip with my ankles.

'Maybe they've got a little saggy with use,' Jess said.

'A little!'

'Still, who's going to see you?'

'Er … you?'

'I'll make a point of not looking.'

I heard her door open. Then I heard her say 'Oh.' Then she said, kind of slowly, 'Jiggy…'

'All right, I'm coming, I'm coming.'

I opened my door, stormed out holding up my elephant drawers with both hands, and headed poolward in a hurry, thinking that I would jump in before Jess got more than a glimpse. I was almost there when I heard a voice that wasn't hers.

'Oh, this is priceless!'

My eyes flipped to the side of the pool where these words had come from. It was PP. And he wasn't alone. Jack and Boz were there. So was Carla. I gurgled with horror. I could have just about stood the men, but the thought of Carla eyeballing me in those things was too much. I tossed myself into the pool, head-first.

And sank.

I remember thinking how warm the water was as I went down. Another thing I remember thinking was that the bottom seemed an awfully long way. This wasn't really surprising, because I'd jumped in the deep end, but I made it all the way to the bottom and then I was standing on my hands with the rest of me drifting somewhere above me. It was only then that I realised that in my haste to get into the water I'd forgotten to take a deep breath first. Deep breaths are kind of useful if you're going into water. As my chest started to expand like I can never get it to do in mirrors, I heard a distant splash. Then I was being gripped by the pits and hauled upward. Then my head was out of the water and I was gasping for the breath I'd missed on the way in. Then Jess was pulling me to the side. Then she was lobbing half of me up onto the blue-green tiles.

I lay there for a bit, breathing hard, chest on the tiles, the rest of me dangling over the edge, caring about nothing except how tasty oxygen was. I noticed that the camera was still filming me, half in the water, half out.

'You're a natural, Jimmy!' PP chortled. 'You'll have 'em in stitches!'

This gave me all the incentive I needed to drag the rest of me out. As I got to my feet I gripped the inflated pantaloons. But there was nothing to grip. I glanced down. The ultra-baggy trunks had abandoned ship. Abandoned me. I looked at the water. There they were, floating happily without me. I was standing on the side of the Next Family's swimming pool without a stitch on. And the camera was getting a lensful of the lot. I mean the *lot*. And not only the camera. The eyes of PP, Jack, Boz, Jess and Carla were strolling over everything I prefer to keep under heavy wraps in public.

'Ulp!' I said, and jumped back into the water.

Once more, I sank to the bottom.

And once more I realised too late that I'd forgotten to take that quite important breath!

Chapter Eight

I spent the rest of the afternoon in my room. Alone. Most of the time I just lay on the bed with my arms under my head, staring at the ceiling, wishing I was back where I belonged. When I heard a knock at my door I didn't answer at first.

'Jiggy, you all right?'

Roo Next.

'Mm!'

'May I come in?'

'Your house,' I muttered.

'Jess told me what happened at the pool,' she said, looking round the door. 'I'm so sorry about those swimming trunks.'

'Not as sorry as me.'

'They belong to James, a friend of Toby's who comes here to swim sometimes. He must have left them last time and forgotten to mention it.'

'Big is he, this friend?'

'Well, let me put it like this. When James jumps in, the water leaves.' She left the door, came over, sat down on the side of the bed.

'Not having a great time of it so far, are you?' she said.

I glanced at the door. 'Are *they* with you?'

'No, they've gone off somewhere. Are they getting to you?'

I pulled a face. 'They're everywhere I am. Usually when I'm doing something I'd rather not be filmed doing.'

'Yes, they are a bit intrusive, aren't they?'

'A bit!'

'You could try taking a leaf out of my book,' she said.

'What leaf's that?'

'Make sure you're seen in your best light when the camera's on you.'

'I don't have a best light.'

'Course you do. Just have to turn it on, that's all.'

'And how do I do that?'

'You keep an eye out for the camera, and whenever it points your way become the person you want people to see, not the caricature that DD seems intent on manufacturing.'

'You mean ... *act*?' I said.

'That's what I'm doing. What Solomon's doing. Jess too.'

'You are? I haven't noticed.'

'Oh, I don't mean we're much different from our usual selves. We're just careful when the camera's about. The kind of reality show we signed up for delights in making fools or monsters of the participants, and – '

'That's what I told my folks. Waste of breath.'

' – and we have no plans to be presented in any light other than one of our choosing. We're using them, Jiggy, not letting them use us.'

I sat up at this. 'I like that,' I said.

'Good. So next time you know a camera's anywhere near you, what are you going to do?'

'Um ... tell me.'

'You're going to make sure that you don't fall into or over anything, or lose any more clothing, or say anything that could make you look bad or foolish.'

'Tricky. I'm so good at those things.'

'Well, become less good at them. Be the Jiggy you want to be, not the Jimmy that DD hopes for.'

'I'd like to see his face if I did that.'

'Well, tomorrow's your first chance. They'll be at school with you. You can start then.'

'School? No, school's over. It's the hols now.'

'Still two days to go at Springhollow,' said Roo. 'And because Toby goes there, you'll have to go too, I'm afraid.'

'Springhollow? Don't think I know it.'

'Really? I thought everyone at least knew *of* Springhollow. Some people are very anti, but it seems to work for my two. Toby likes it so much that he's asked to become a boarder from September, even though it's only just down the road.'

At dinner that night, I started to think that maybe I could get used to the food that was served to the Next Family. I didn't know what some of it was, but it was quite tasty, and there was the bonus that it never came with veg. I didn't have to have fruit afterwards either. My mum's always trying to stuff fruit down me after meals when all I want is chocolate or ice-cream or cake, like a caring mother would let you have.

Just before sloping up to bed I went to see Hector. Even though there were all those other rabbits in the cage with him, he came straight to the wire when I looked in. I undid the gate very carefully so none of the others could escape, and reached in for him. When I lifted him out he snuggled up like he really loved me. Holding him with his warm fur and his big eyes and twitchy little nose, I felt better than I had since this TV thing started. Tomorrow I'd have to go to school with Jess, and PP and Jack the cameraman were going to be there, but I liked Roo's advice about showing myself the way I wanted to be seen, not the way they wanted. Yes, I thought, I'll do that. Tomorrow, at Jess's school, I won't be Jimmy the Saddo, I'll be Cool Jig McCue, Actorrr.

Chapter Nine

When I woke up next morning there was a spot on my right cheek. It wasn't a huge spot, but it was still a spot, which wasn't good news because when I get spots they grow like radishes and there's absolutely no pretending they're not there. Unless luck was on my side for a change – ha! – this one would take over the entire advertising space above my neck in days.

Spot or no spot, though, I had to go to school with Jess.

Springhollow – which Roo drove us to – was a very different kind of school to Ranting Lane, where I spend most of my life. The main building was like one of those stately homes your parents drag you to every time someone drops a hat. It was a huge house with ivy and wide staircases and lots of rooms that didn't look like classrooms. There was a lot of ground too, with ancient trees and a couple of tennis courts, even a crazy-golf course, but no playground. Kids of all ages walked around or sat on the grass or rode bikes, and none of them wore school uniform.

'Hi, Joe,' Jess said to a Golden Oldie in jeans and an Iron Maiden T-shirt who sat with his back against a tree doing a crossword.

He looked up. 'Hi, Jess. Who's this?'

'Jiggy McCue. He's staying with us for a couple of weeks. Taking Toby's place here till we finish.'

'Oh, it's that swap thing you mentioned.'

'Yeah. The TV people are filming us here today.'

Joe raised an arm with a fist on the end. 'Good to meet you, Jiggy.'

I looked at the fist, then got what it was for. I bunched one of mine and touched knuckles.

'Joe teaches English,' Jess said to me.

'I'd do a better job if you brats turned up more often,' said Joe, getting up and dusting his behind with his paper. 'There's a session after the meeting if you're interested.'

'See how I feel,' she said.

Joe nodded, folded his paper, and stuffed it in a back pocket. 'Right you are. See you, Jiggy.'

As he headed for the house and we carried on across the grass, I said, 'See how you *feel*? He doesn't mind if you skip lessons?'

'It's up to us,' she said. 'They're big on personal choice at Springhollow. Hey, the crew's arrived.'

She meant the TV van, which contained Jack and Boz. PP's flash sports car pulled up behind them. Carla was in the passenger seat. When I saw her I swerved behind a tree. Carla! How could I face her after yesterday at the pool? It was bad enough being with Jess, but *Carla*!

Jess joined me behind the tree. 'What's up?'

'I don't want to see them yet.'

'But they're here to film us. We can't avoid them all day.'

'Later. Not now.'

'Well, I suppose we could sneak into the meeting by the side door and keep our heads down. Hey, there's a couple of my mates. Maybe they...' She leaned out from the tree. 'Pol!' she said in a stage whisper. 'Sal!'

Pol had green sticky-up hair and Sal wore huge dangly earrings. They both wore bright red nail polish and lip-gloss. What sort of school *was* this? They came to the tree, where Jess told them who I was. They looked me over like I was something stuck to a sheep's backside.

'Toby's been swapped for *him*?' the one called Sal said, eyeing me down her nose. She was taller than me. All three of them were taller than me.

'Bit down the food chain,' said the other girl, Pol.

'He's from the Brook Farm Estate,' Jess said, like where I was from made a difference.

'Well so are Roberta Petheridge and Natalie Breen, but...'

'From the shopping centre side,' she added.

'Aaah,' said Pol and Sal, swapping 'that-explains-everything' glances.

'Remember I told you a film crew would be here today?' Jess said. They said they remembered. 'Well, they've just got here but we're not ready for them. Can you cover us to the library?'

'Cover you?'

'Act as a barrier for us.'

She organised her snooty pals so they walked between us and the crew to a side entrance of the house. From there the four of us went along a hallway to this big room – a library with tall bookcases and couches and armchairs where people could sit and read. Kids from about seven to seventeen, and a smattering of Golden Oldies, sat on the couches or chairs, or a flight of stairs going up to another level. The rest sprawled on the floor or just stood around. Pol and Sal darted off to talk to some other girls and Jess found us a couple of chairs.

'What's this meeting?' I asked as we sat down.

'We have three a week usually,' she said. 'Monday, Wednesday and Friday mornings. The meetings are where we make the laws, sort out disputes and grievances and stuff.'

'Laws?'

'Yeah. Have to be laws or the place'd fall apart.'

'Golden Oldie laws, naturally,' I said.

'Golden Oldie?'

'Adults.'

'Not just them. Everyone's in on the decision-making. Laws can be proposed by anyone, any age, and they're passed by majority vote. Might not be any new ones today though, it being the last meeting of term.'

'What sort of laws are these?'

'Oh, for-or-against laws about skinny-dipping in the pool, what to do with anyone caught stealing, music played after lights out, that sort of thing.'

I thought how I wouldn't mind proposing a few laws at Ranting Lane. First up would be an end to Maths, History, PE and compulsory Sport. That would mean bye-bye Mr Dakin, Mr Hurley and

Mr Rice, and yippees all round, specially from me.

Suddenly one of the older boys rang a hand-bell.

'That's Tanesh,' Jess said. 'This month's chairperson. He's calling the meeting to order. The chair has absolute power in the meetings. If you don't keep quiet he can fine you or tell you to leave.'

'Even the teachers?'

'Even the teachers.'

'What are they like, your teachers? That one we met seemed OK.'

'They're all OK. They only hire nice people to teach here.'

'Don't any of them shout at you?'

'Shout? If they did they'd probably be voted out.'

'And that would mean...?'

'They'd have to find a job somewhere else.'

'How do I get into this school?' I asked eagerly.

'You have to pay.'

I de-eagered. 'Well, that's that then.'

'Better shut up now or we could be kicked out ourselves.'

There'd been some laughter and chat after the bell went, but the room was almost silent now. The boy called Tanesh started speaking.

'Last meeting of term, so let's keep it sweet, shall we?' he said. 'To kick off, any new issues?'

Three hands went up. One was an adult's. Tanesh pointed to one of the kids, a boy of about my age.

'The radiator by my bed's still on at night, even though it's supposed to have been adjusted,' the boy said. 'It was so hot last night I hardly slept a wink.'

Tanesh looked at a man sitting on the stairs with a bunch of kids.

'Roger?'

'I'll sort it, right after this,' Roger said. 'Some of the rads are stone-age. Probably a dodgy valve.'

Tanesh pointed to the adult who'd raised a mitt.

'Eric?'

'There were wheel tracks in the hall on Friday. Mrs Darkis had a go at me like it was my fault.'

'Anyone care to own up to that?' Tanesh asked.

There was a pause. Then another Golden Oldie hand went up. 'Sorry. Slow puncture, and I was late in. Didn't think I left tracks.'

'That's Ted Smart, the Head,' Jess whispered in my ear.

'You know the rule, Ted,' Tanesh said. 'Bike indoors, fiver in the kitty.'

'Fair do's,' said Ted.

'And don't do it again please.'

'At a fiver a time, you can count on it.'

I turned to Jess in amazement. 'He just called the headmaster by his first name, and told him off, and *fined* him,' I whispered.

'Quite right too,' she whispered back. 'Ted should know better, specially as he voted for the no-bikes-indoors law.'

There were a few other small complaints and then Tanesh asked if anyone wanted to propose any new laws. When no one did, he asked if anyone wanted to scrap any old ones. Several kids and one adult did, people voted, and three old laws were abolished, just like that.

'Any other business?' Tanesh said then.

There wasn't, so he called an end to the meeting. People started to get up.

'Wait! Please!'

All eyes flipped doorward. PP stood there. I groaned. He told everyone who he was, that he had a cameraman with him, and that he wanted us to act like the meeting was still happening so he could film it. He had a quick word with Ted the Head, who must have already been told there was going to be filming because he didn't look fazed. I didn't think PP had seen Jess and me but he had, because he came over, smiling that big phoney smile of his so everyone could see what a charming person he was.

'I wish you two'd told us where to find you,' he said, leaning over us. 'This is a big place.'

'Sorry, didn't think of it,' said Jess.

'OK, but stand up, will you, so Jack can get you in frame.'

I looked towards the door. Jack was there now, with Boz and their camera equipment. And Carla.

PP asked Tanesh to act like he was just starting the meeting, which he did as soon as Jack said he was ready to film. They did three takes before PP was satisfied. Jess and I didn't have to say or do anything during this, just stand in the crowd. When he'd got everything he wanted, PP thanked everyone and we all started to leave. Jess and I were the only ones who didn't make it out of there.

'Need to get some footage of you two in class,' PP said to us, blocking our way. 'And maybe having lunch later, and sitting around outside. Nothing dramatic, just a spot of padding.'

Jess said 'fine' and I sort of nodded, deliberately not looking at Carla, standing nearby.

'Hi, Jimmy.'

I grunted and started past her, but she touched my arm and lightning ziggered up it and exploded in my chest.

'Walk with me while DD sets up the classroom scene,' she whispered in one of my suddenly burning lugs.

My Adam's apple jumped so high it almost cut off my air supply. The way she *said* that! I chanced a glance at the eyes I'd been trying to avoid. They were bigger and greener than ever today. And they were looking into mine. *Right* into mine.

'Sure...'

'What about me?' Jess said.

Carla smiled at her. 'We'll see you in class.'

'Which class?'

'Whichever you go to from here.'

'Have I really got to be there?'

'If you don't mind.'

Jess turned to me. 'Looks like I'm doing English like it or not.'

Carla guided my arm to the main door of the house and away across the grounds. I walked like something out of a field with wooden legs. She walked like a fantastically gorgeous girl on wheels.

In a minute she said: 'Something bothering you, Jimmy?'

Jimmy, Jimmy, always Jimmy. But somehow when she said it my hackles didn't rise. In fact, because she called me it I considered changing my name by deed poll. I tried to get a grip on myself. I had to play it cooler than this.

'Bothering me?' I said smoothly, wishing I'd seen more James Bond films.

She stopped suddenly under this big tree, and I stopped too, mainly because she was still holding my arm. She turned me to face her.

'It's not that business at the pool yesterday, is it?'

'Pool?' This came out about six octaves higher than I meant it to. So much for smooth.

'It is, isn't it?'

And her terrific green eyes came over all soft and melty, and... (gulp) she touched my cheek. The spotless one.

'Silly boy,' she said. 'I haven't given it a moment's thought.'

'You haven't?'

'No. And neither must you. You have an

important job to do here. You're a star of a big television programme. What does a little thing like that matter?'

The 'little thing' was a bit personal, but I let it go because my head was spinning like a plate on a stick. She'd taken hold of both my elbows to say it, and her face was less than two noses from mine.

'Now I want you to do something for me,' she said, softly.

'Wossat 'en?' I asked, for some reason turning into Eejit Atkins.

'I want you to get through the day's filming without worrying about anything, and after that...'

'After that?'

'Well.' She gave me a shy little smile and fluttered her eyelashes at me. 'We'll have to see, won't we?'

I would have replied, would have said, 'Will we?' but my tongue had stapled itself to the roof of my mouth. She seemed to get it though.

'We will,' she said. 'But in the meantime...'

She let go of my elbows and my arms fell to my sides like lead drainpipes. She felt in her purse and took out a little box. She opened the box. Inside was a tiny red rose made of metal.

'In the meantime I'd like you to wear this.'

She fixed the little rose to my shirt, just above where my heart was heaving like a concrete mixer. She was giving me a gift. A lapel pin. A personal pin, from her to me.

'Will you keep it on?' she said. 'For me?'

'You bet,' I said, thinking that if it had been the Saturday after next I'd even wear it in the bath.

She gave me a big toothy smile and took my arm again – the opposite arm to the one she'd used to walk me to the tree – and we strolled back to the school. And you know what? I wasn't all stiff-legged any more. I was walking almost like a normal person, but on air. I nodded to myself. The day was mine. And so was the girl. Or she would be once the filming was over and done with. After all, she wasn't that much older than me. Four years, five max. What does age matter when you're in love?

Chapter Ten

Jess's English lesson wasn't much different to English at Ranting Lane except it was more relaxed and aimed at kids her age, not mine. I'm good at English, though, so I had no trouble keeping up. Apart from the TV people there were just seven of us in the classroom – me, Jess, four others, and Joe the teacher. Joe didn't seem bothered about the pupil famine. He even said it was a pretty good turnout for the last day but one.

PP told everyone to carry on as if he and his team were invisible. Joe managed this, so did Jess and I, but the other kids kept looking at the camera because they weren't professionals like us. I had a hard time keeping my eyes off Carla. Every time mine met hers she gave me this wow of a smile that made me go all ripply inside. Because she was there I put on a good show when Joe asked the class some language questions. I could tell she was impressed. PP wasn't, though, and I knew why. He'd decided the way he wanted me to look in his film (moody, curling my lip, falling A over T into something disgusting). What he did not want was me being bright in class. Being bright in class didn't make fun television. Oh, I'd got his number.

There was a bit more not-very-interesting filming of Jess and me later, this time scoffing sandwiches outside on the grass.

'What, no pills and bog juice?' I said to Jess.

'Only when we're at home,' she explained. 'We bring special Sans-earthist sandwiches to school. Mrs Moult makes them.'

I pulled my two slices of brown bread apart. It looked like chicken in there.

'What's a Sans-earthist sandwich?'

'One that doesn't contain anything earth-grown.'

'What about the bread? Bread has to have flour in it, and flour comes from wheat and stuff – doesn't it?'

'Our bread doesn't contain flour,' she said.

'What's it made from then?'

'No idea. Don't care. Hasn't killed any of us yet.'

I nibbled a corner of my sandwich. It was a bit tougher than the bread I was used to, a bit chewier, but it wasn't bad.

When PP had got all he wanted of us eating,

he and the others went off to get some lunch at a pub. I asked Jess what lessons there were that afternoon.

'Well, there's drama and history,' she said. 'But it's too nice to go to them. Let's just relax.'

'Have we got to do it here?'

'Do what here?'

'Relax. I mean, can't we just go home?'

'No. One of the school laws. Students have to stay on the premises between first and last bells, even if they spend the time playing crazy-golf or dozing with a magazine over their faces.'

So we stayed there for a while, sprawling on the grass, and then we walked about for a bit because it was a warm day and I can't do sun-sprawling on warm days for long. We weren't the only ones not to go to lessons. There were kids all over the grounds, playing games, riding bikes and skateboards, kicking balls about, climbing up to a tree-house that looked pretty unsafe to me. Some were smoking. And not just the older kids.

'Don't tell me that's allowed,' I said.

'Smoking? Sure, why not?'

'Well, it's still a school. And some of them can't be much more than eleven.'

Jess shrugged. 'They've been shown the anti-smoking films, heard the health warnings. It's up to them if they want to smoke regardless, long as they do it out of doors and don't leave their dog-ends behind.'

'Is there anything you *can't* get away with here?' I asked.

'Well, they don't approve of stealing, doing drugs or being drunk too often in class.'

'Drunk too *often*?'

'Yeah, some of these teachers. Hey, I fancy a drag myself actually. Let's get in the shade.'

She led the way to this tumbly old ruin over to one side of the grounds. Looked like it was quite a big place once, but now it was just stretches of bumpy wall and rows of stones. No roof. I asked Jess what it was before it crumbled.

'Thirteenth century chapel,' she said. 'But it didn't crumble, it burned down a coupla years ago. Mystery what started it.'

'Probably a bunch of you smokers,' I said.

Inside the remains of the old chapel we flopped in the shadow of a high stretch of wall and Jess whipped out a pack of cigarettes. She offered me one. I shook my head.

'Don't you ever?' she said.

'No, never fancied it. Think my dad put me off.'

'What, he told you it was bad for you?'

'No, he smoked like a chimney, always, till I was about ten, when Mum said that if he kept on he'd have to do it outside.'

'And he gave up, just like that?'

'No, he smoked in the garden. But one night – dead of winter, really cold, ice on the windows, the works – Mum locked the back and front doors not knowing he wasn't in. I was up in my room with my headphones on and she turned the telly up to watch a programme about dysfunctional families and fell asleep, so neither of us heard him hammering. She found him just before bedtime, on the back step, mouth frozen to the cat-flap. His lips were in plaster for a week. Hasn't touched a fag since, far as I know.'

While I told this sorry tale, Jess lit up and got down to some serious puffing. She blew some neat smoke rings. I always wanted to do that, but without using cigarettes. Then I remembered something.

'Your lot don't touch anything that comes from the earth, your mum said. Tobacco's grown in the earth. Or is it just things you eat?'

'No, tobacco's included. Mum and Dad don't know I smoke.'

'Can't they smell it on your clothes?'

'I spray myself with smoke neutraliser before I go home.'

'Hey, Jessie.'

Her nose-in-the-air buds Sal and Pol had strolled round the wall with a couple of friends. One of the new girls wanted to know who I was and when Jess told them they tried to act like it was uncool to be interested in the Kid Swap thing and changed the subject to nothing much. When the four of them sat down with us I was sort of in the middle and felt surrounded, and when they all lit up too I was suddenly breathing smoke from all directions. Pol asked Jess why I wasn't smoking.

'Cos he doesn't,' she said.

The girl called Sal flipped out an extra cig. 'Try it,' she said to me.

'No thanks.'

'Oh, go on.'

'No.'

'I *insist*,' she said, leaning closer, face all tight.

'No. Really. I don't wa—'

I stopped because she'd jammed the cig between

my teeth and was already putting a lighter flame to the end of it. I gasped, and when I gasped I was instantly full of smoke and struggling for breath. I tore the cigarette from my mouth, but it was too late, I was coughing like a maniac and the girls were roaring with laughter. I think I even heard Jess's giggle in there somewhere, but I couldn't see properly through the water in my eyes.

It wasn't until I'd got over the worst of the coughing that I thought to drop the cig. Then I jumped to my feet and stamped on it again and again. I was shouting too, but don't ask me what, I was too mad to pay attention.

'Hey, Jig, calm down, it was a joke.' This was definitely Jess.

'Get lost!' I said, and stormed off.

I was almost at the end of the wall we'd been sitting against when I saw PP and Jack. They'd slyly filmed me smoking and coughing my guts up. So much for me acting cool. I ran to the school gates and out into the street. I didn't care if I wasn't supposed to leave till the bell went. I'd had it with school. All schools. At least until September.

Chapter eleven

As I didn't have a driver I had to walk back to the Next house from Springhollow. It was further than I usually like to walk in one go, but it gave me time to calm down and jam some clean air into my lungs. I could still taste the smoke, and my throat felt dryer than sand, but I didn't have a drink with me so I had to put up with it.

When I reached the house I knocked on the front door. Betty the maid let me in. She was surprised to see me.

'I thought you were at school,' she said.

'I hate school,' I grouched.

'Even Springhollow?'

'Specially Springhollow.'

I noticed her nose wrinkle and knew that she'd smelt smoke on me. She gave me an 'I-know-what-you've-been-doing' look but didn't say it.

I went up to my room, put the chair against the door, stripped off, and for the fourth unbelievable time in two days took a shower. Afterwards I wiped the steam off the mirror over the basin to see if my spot had gone down. Some hopes. It had grown, and was even redder than before. Worse still there were all these other little bumps too now. Baby spots getting set to punch their way out and grow gigantic.

When I'd put on some of the other togs my mother had ironed and packed for me, I lay on the bed not caring if I wrinkled them. I turned the TV on, flipped through five million channels, found nothing worth watching, and turned it off again. After that I must have snoozed because I definitely wasn't awake before a car pulled up on the gravel below my window. I got up and went to see who it was. Roo, bringing Jess home. I hoped Betty wouldn't tell them where I was. I didn't need questions and chat right now. What I needed was a silent cuddle from someone who loved me and didn't expect me to do anything I didn't want.

Hector.

I waited till Roo and Jess were indoors, then crept downstairs. They were talking in a room off the hall, but I managed to sneak by and out the front door. I went round the back of the house to where the big rabbit cage was. I looked in, couldn't see Hector, but it was pretty crowded in there. I stretched my neck and looked harder, but still couldn't see his rusty fur. Maybe he's been moved to a more personal cage now that he's mine and has a name, I thought.

'Hey, Jig.'

I turned. Jess.

'How did you know I was here?'

'Saw you come this way. You walk home?'

'Yeh. Where's Hector?'

'Who?'

'My rabbit.'

'Oh, Mrs Moult's seeing to him. Look, I'm sorry about what happened. The girls were only fooling around.'

'Yeah, you said.'

'I shouldn't have let them.'

'Mm.'

I walked away. I was still too mad to talk about it. Hoped she picked up the vibe.

I stayed in my room until dinner time, and even then I didn't go down right away. After a while Jess came up and tapped.

'Nosh time, Jig,' she said through the door.

I sighed. She'd apologised. Time had passed. I ought to let it go.

''Kay.'

I got off the bed and opened the door.

'I really am sorry about what happened,' she said.

I told her to forget it and we went downstairs.

Solomon and Roo were already at the table. They sat at opposite ends as usual. Jess and I took our places across from one another. There was a bit of chat about the filming and stuff, then Mrs Moult and Betty brought the plates in. Each plate contained a mound of dark meat surrounded by what looked like AstroTurf.

'What is it?' I asked.

'Rabbit,' said Mrs Moult, not meaning the AstroTurf.

I stared at the plate in front of me. 'Rabbit?'

'Very young, very fresh. Killed just this afternoon.'

'Killed?'

'You have to kill animals to eat them,' Roo said.

'I know, but...'

'Simple fact of life, Jimmy,' said Solomon.

'Jiggy,' said Jess.

'Yes, sorry. Law of the jungle, Jiggy. Kill or be killed.'

'I don't think rabbits would leave their hutches and hunt us,' I said.

He chuckled. 'We didn't hunt these. We bought them to eat.'

'When you say "bought them"...'

'You met them yesterday,' Jess said.

'I met your *pet* rabbits yesterday,' I reminded her.

She frowned. 'Pet rabbits? I never said they were pets.'

'We don't keep pets,' said Solomon.

'What about the horses?' I said.

'The horses serve a purpose. When they're past it we'll shove 'em on a roasting spit and buy a couple more.'

I looked at Jess. 'Even Genevieve?'

'Even Genevieve,' she said. 'Maybe I shouldn't have named her, but when you spend as much time with an animal as I do with her it's hard not to call them something.'

I had a sudden thought. Not a good one.

'The rabbit you gave me. Hector. He's still mine, isn't he?'

Jess smiled. 'Still yours? What do you think that is?'

She was looking at my plate. At the mound of dark meat.

'This isn't him?'

'Course it is! I asked you to choose the one you wanted, and he was the one you picked. Tuck in, Jig!'

Chapter Twelve

That night I had a nightmare. It wasn't one of those utterly terrifying eleven-out-of-ten nightmares, but it was bad enough to jerk me awake all in a sweat. I was in this big cage full of straw with Jess and her brother and Pete (in the n-mare), and a few other kids who didn't seem to have faces. I don't think Angie was there. Suddenly someone much bigger than us was looking in. Carla. And she was holding Hector, my cooked rabbit, who was glaring at me accusingly and had a cigarette in his mouth. Smoke-rings were rising from Hector's cig and breaking up as they hit the wire of the cage, making all of us inside cough like crazy, even the ones without faces. I think I was coughing myself when I did the jerk-awake-in-a-sweat bit.

Lying there panting after the nightmare I wished more than ever that I was back home in my own bed. When I have a nightmare at home I sometimes go to my parents' room and shake their shoulders with the idea of sharing it with them. Dad usually growls something like, 'Jig, couldn't you tell us in the *morning*?' and slaps a pillow over his head, but Mum's almost always more sympathetic. Always has been, even if she is perfectly happy to hand me over to another family the moment the housekeeping runs a bit low.

A little later, when Jess knocked on my door to tell me to come down for breakfast because her mum was running us to school soon, I put on the feeble act my mum's such a sucker for when I want to get off school.

'You're not well?' Jess said through the wood.

'Noooooo,' I croaked, ruffling my hair a second before she came in.

'What's wrong?'

'Feel terrible. Could be something I ate. Or smoked.'

'Maybe you'd better stay in bed today then.'

'Mmmmm.'

'Should I ask Mrs Moult for some meds?'

'No. I'll sleep it off.'

'OK. See you after school. Hope you feel better soon.'

She closed the door and I kept to the mattress till I heard her mum's car go, then I shuffled into the en-suite for a widdle. I was washing my hands afterwards when I glanced in the mirror over the basin and almost hit the wall behind me in shock. There were now five spots. And they weren't starter-spots. They must have been working away all night to break out while I had cosy nightmares about smoking rabbits and Carla. I gasped. Carla! If she saw me like this she'd reach for a big wooden cross and fling an arm across her eyes. Ah, but would she be around today? Maybe not. As she was PP's assistant she'd probably be wherever he was, and I reckoned that would be either at my house on Brook Farm or at Springhollow expecting to get some more bad stuff of me. If they went to Springhollow Jess would tell them I was sick and they would leave me in peace for the day – wouldn't they? If they did, if they stayed clear of the house, maybe the spots would be gone by tomorrow.

As if.

Once spots stake a claim on my face they have a way of growing to the size of small mountains while I blink. My head can look like a lunar landscape illuminated by bright red 'spotlights', and unless I squeeze them out in the mirror it can be a week before they sink back under the skin. I really didn't need this now, now of all times, when I was being filmed for half the nation's couch spudatoes to leer at over the pizzas and sardine masalas they've just had delivered. I also didn't want Carla to see me like that. Her most of all. So what could I do? I had to cover the spots up. But what with? I looked along the shelf behind the basin, hoping to find some tube or pot that screamed 'TOTAL SPOT DESTROYER', but there was nothing like that. Toby probably never got spots. He sounded too *perfect* to get spots.

There was only one thing in the en-suite that might do the business. Talcum powder. I tipped some into my hand and patted my face. Quite a lot fell onto the front of my pyjama jacket, which was dark blue with light blue squares, but at least the spots didn't look so bad now. All right, I looked like the ghost of someone who died in his sleep, but you can't have everything. I went back to bed.

While lying on my back to give the talc a chance to sink into the spots, my mind turned back to Carla. I sighed and reached to the bedside table for the little rose pin she'd given me, and kissed it (pin, not table). I thought of her eyes and hair and face, and sighed again. I'd known quite a lot of girls with eyes, hair and faces, but most of them were nothing special. There'd only been a couple I really liked in a hyper sort of way. Dawn Overton from next door was one, but I'd got over her. Another was Ayesha Bandari, who joined my class last term. I didn't notice Ayesha at first. Why would I? Half the class were girls. You don't spend any more time noticing them than you do listening to the teachers. But one day I looked up from doodling on my desk instead of wasting ear time on Mr Hurley chuntering about something Historic, and caught her eyeballing me. Then I looked up a while later and she was doing it again. 'What's she gawping at?' I thought, getting back to some heavy doodling. But this kept on happening, and after a while I started to miss it when I looked up and she wasn't ogling me. After that lesson I started hanging back at the end of the afternoon, hoping to bump into her, or looked for her before school, and if I saw her I got kind of loud and show-offy so she'd think I was cool. At night she was in my brain when I went to sleep, and still there when I woke up, and I couldn't eat properly. This went on for weeks and we never said a word to one another, but then

I finally worked up the nerve to speak to her, and waited the other side of a corner I knew she'd be round any minute. And round she came – arm-in-arm with Bryan Ryan, archest of all my enemies! As they passed me she caught my eye one final time and shrugged sadly as if to say 'Well, I couldn't wait *forever.*' The heartbreak lasted for seven whole days. Maybe seven and a half. That's the last time I encourage a female type, I thought. But now there was Carla. So much for resolutions.

About an hour after she drove Jess to school, her mum came up and knocked on my door.

'Jiggy?'

'Eeeeeegh?' I groaned, piling it on something rotten.

'Are you all right?'

'Eeergh.'

The door started to open. I pulled the duvet up to my chin, jerked my mouth corners down, and half-closed my eyes and tried to make my eyes look unfocused.

'Oh, my God!'

Roo came in. Stood over the bed looking down at me.

'You are so *white*!' she said.

My first thought was that this was a bit racist, but then I remembered the talcum powder. I moved my lips like they were made of solid oak, and slipped a couple of faint heroic words past them.

'It's... nothing...'

Roo's eyes melted. Well, not exactly melted, or they'd have run down her cheeks. I mean she came over all sympathetic.

'What on earth *is* it?' she wondered.

'Some... bug... maybe,' I suggested feebly.

'I'd better call Dr Seuss.'

'Dr who?' I said, startled.

'No, Dr Seuss. Yes, I know, but he can't help it, he's Austrian.'

'No,' I said. 'No doctor. I'll... be... all right.'

'It could be something serious,' Roo said. 'Do you want something to eat or drink while we're waiting for him?'

'No. And I really don't want a doctor.'

'Well you're getting one,' she said, and headed for the door.

At another time I might have asked her to tell the doc not to forget his cat and his hat, but this wasn't another time. *Now what?* I thought when I was alone again. Even a doctor with a name like that

111

would know I wasn't really ill. Probably. I'd fooled our own doc more than once, but that could be because Dr Wolfe is a quack. I sometimes wonder if he's actually qualified because whenever he prescribes something for a member of my family it makes us worse, or has side-effects we could do without. Mum once had an itchy neck and he gave her some cream that made her talk in a loud screechy voice and still didn't cure the neck. Another time, Dad went to him with a bad knee and ended up at the hospital having his brain scanned.*

But maybe this Dr Seuss wasn't like Dr Wolfe. Maybe he knew his onions. Dr Wolfe tries to worm his way out of house calls, but if Roo knew that Dr Seuss would visit if she called him I guessed that he was a private doctor whose time she'd have to pay through the ear, nose and throat for. If he was keen to show that he was worth the money he might want to diagnose what was wrong with me so it would look good on the receipt. Except there was nothing wrong with me. So...

I had to get better. And soon. I'd only pretended to be ill to get out of going to school anyway, and I'd done that, so maybe it was time for a miracle cure. I lay there for some time wondering how to

---

* They gave up. Couldn't find one.

look like I was getting better. I couldn't look *totally* better, just had to seem better enough to not be bounced up one-way streets the wrong way in the back of a paranoid ambulance with a tube up my snout.

I got out of bed and went to check my appearance in the en-suite mirror. My face looked like a death mask with lumps. I ran the tap and dabbed my skin with my finger-ends. Wherever I dabbed, the talc dissolved. Time to use the new flannel my mother had bought and packed for me. I dampened it and wiped the rest of the talc off, except where it clung to the spots. Then I started on those too, super-carefully – dab-dab, dab-dab-dab – until they were also talc-free. Unfortunately, when it was all gone my spots looked even redder than before. Maybe they were allergic to talcum powder.

Another major downside to removing the talc was that I no longer looked even a bit sick. Just spotty. I needed to look like I'd been unwell but was over the worst of it, so what could I...?

Ah! Toothpaste.

I squirted a glob onto a finger and pasted it under my eyes. Not bad. The red stripes helped. I added a drop of water and moved the stripes around so they looked sort of veiny. Then I tapped the area with a towel corner and stood back to get a visitor's view of the result. The streaky red under-eye circles *might* fool a non-quacking doctor, but maybe I needed to look a bit sweaty too, as if I'd been suffering before he walked in. How could I do that? Vaseline? It was colourless and shone when the light hit it, so maybe. There was a jar of the stuff in the little bathroom cupboard. I stuck my fingers in and smeared some on my cheeks. The result wasn't great. Looked like smeared Vaseline. I wiped it off and ran my fingers through my hair to get rid of the rest. Now I looked like someone with measles who was experimenting with a new hairdo.

I was back where I started, wondering how I could get the all-over sweat look without taking a nap and having another quick nightmare. How *do* people get sweaty? Well, if they're out on a really hot day they might get a shine without much trouble, but the sun wasn't hanging from my ceiling so that was out. If they sit too close to a blazing fire they might also gleam a bit, but there wasn't a blazing fire in the room. Of course, if they exercise like mental zombies they work up a lather, but you need a gym for that... don't you?

Now I hate exercise. Exercise is what you're forced to do on school playing fields and in places with parallel bars while cretins in red tracksuits scream 'Try harder, McCue, *harder*, lad!' But maybe, just this once, I could do a little. It was a good cause after all. OK, so how little exercise could I get away with and still raise a sweat? I sat down and tried thumb wrestling myself, but didn't even get warm. I ran to the bed and flopped on it. Nothing. I tried running on the spot for five seconds (quietly, so no one would hear downstairs). Zippo.

I had to think again.

I looked around. There wasn't enough room for a hundred metre dash, or a high-jump session, or a long-jump unless I wanted to go out the window. There wasn't the equipment for rope-climbing either, or horse-vaulting, or failing to stop balls kicked into footie nets by morons. Which left what exactly? What could I do in a confined space that would make me break out in a...

Oh. Of course. Press-ups.

I know I said I hate exercise, but of all kinds of exercise I hate press-ups the most. Press-ups give my shoulders a headache and make me feel faint. I always try to get out of them when Mr Rice orders us to do them. I say I've sprained a wrist or something. He never buys it. But the doc could be here any time and I couldn't think of another way to look like a person who's getting over a sick spell, so I slotted myself into the space between the bed and the door, stretched out, and got started. Feet standing on bent toes, palms flat on the floor below my shoulders, elbows bending like electric hairpins, up-down I went. Up-down, up-down, faster, faster, up-down, up-down, never-again, up-down, up-down, faster, up-down. Soon I could feel myself getting warm. A few more minutes and I'd look like I'd been caught in a sudden downpour. I just hoped the doc arrived before I went into a coma. Up-down, up-down, up-dow—

'Jiggy, what...?'

I froze in a high press-up. Craned my neck. Roo and the doctor stared at me from the door.

'I'm... trying... to get... better,' I gasped breathlessly.

Chapter Thirteen

Dr Seuss had one of those long, bony faces that doesn't seem to like anything much. He didn't seem to take to me, that's for sure. Looked at me like he thought I was just another time-wasting brat on a mat. But he got me on the bed, felt my pulse, went over me with a stethoscope made of ice, thumbed my eyelids, and took my blood pressure (probably all ways of bumping up his fee). He seemed a bit suspicious of the red toothpaste streaks under my eyes, but didn't comment on them. He didn't say what he thought might be wrong with me either, but when he said, 'Well, I'll write a prescription,' he said it all sort of wearily, like there was no point cashing it in. I thought of trying to liven things up with, 'Can I have it as a pill, can I have it cos I'm ill?', but managed not to.

After she'd seen him off, Roo drove to the nearest pharmacy and came back with some medicine, which I had to take because she brought a spoon with it, filled it, and held it to my lips until they parted. It was disgusting. I bet the doc had chosen the worst-tasting most useless medicine he could think of to teach me a lesson for being a boy. Then Roo slotted me into her son's dressing gown and led me downstairs like I was your average ninety-six-year-old who's pawned his Zimmer to pay the gas.

She guided me to the kitchen and went to find Mrs Moult to get me something to eat. While I was waiting, my eyes trotted along the shelves of kitcheny things for the exercise. They didn't see much of interest until they hit a packet of custard powder. *Ah-ha*, I thought to myself. *Custard powder. Not as white as talcum or as streaky as the toothpaste. Maybe it'll help conceal the spots when the camera aims at me next time, or when I next see Carla.* I looked over my shoulder. No one there. (Always a relief, that.) I looked over the other one. Ditto. I got up, took four steps, whipped the packet of custard powder off the shelf, stuffed it in my pocket, and sat down a split second before Mrs Moult came in.

'What's all this, Master Jiggy?' she said. 'Not feeling so sturdy? What you need is some of Mother Moult's Home-Made Soup!'

She went to the fridge, took out a big bowl, and ladled some of her soup into a saucepan. When it was warmed through, she poured the soup into a smaller bowl and told me to get it down me (the soup, not the bowl). I dipped my spoon in while she watched with her arms folded across her big bosom. I don't know what flavour the soup was – could've been Speckled Toad & Roadkill for all I know – but it tasted pretty good. I was still sipping from the spoon like a really ancient person when I heard hushed voices from the doorway. I glanced towards them. I was being filmed.

'Ignore us,' said PP.

I cursed under my breath. I hadn't had a chance to slap custard powder on my spots. But remembering that I was an Actorrr I hunched further over my bowl and made it look like it was a real task to hoist that spoon. I was still doing this when Roo returned. She walked in like the camera wasn't there and congratulated me on finishing most of the soup as she helped me out of the chair and led me to the door. I knew the camera was still following us as we went along the hall, but this time I only walked like an eighty-four year old to show how much better I was feeling after the soup. Roo showed me into the little room they called 'the snug', which I hadn't been in before. In the snug there were pictures on walls, books on shelves, a couple of big soft couches and some fluffy rugs. Nice room. Roo led me to one of the couches and covered me with a blanket from somewhere and told me to 'lie quiet', which seemed a good plan for someone who doesn't know how to lie noisy. The camera had followed us to the doorway and was still on me as I settled down under the blanket, but before she left me Roo said to PP and Jack: 'That's enough for now, the lad needs his rest,' and closed the door, shutting them out.

It was so cosy in that room – the regular clunk-clunk-clunk of the clock on the mantelpiece helped – that I soon got drowsy. And snoozed. I don't know how long I was out, but I was woken by a tap at the window. I cranked the McCue lids up to see what was tapping.

'Jimmy!' PP shouted through the glass. 'Stagger this way looking like you're about to kick the proverbial bucket, will you?'

I didn't go to the window kicking buckets, even proverbial ones. I slid off the couch and went up to my room, where I jammed the chair under the door handle to stop them following me. Then I climbed onto the bed and sank back into snooze mode.

Jess came up after school, which had ended early as it was the last day of term. She asked if I was awake through the door. When I said that I wasn't she said she'd got a mug of Bovril for me and I told her to come in – feebly of course.

'Can't get in!' she yelled.

'Oh yeah, forgot!'

I swung off the bed, whipped the chair from the handle, opened up.

'Why'd you block the door?' she asked as she came in.

'To keep you-know-who out.' I took the mug of Bovril – 'Thanks, I'm starving!' – tilted it to my lips, and shrieked because my mouth had just caught fire.

'You don't seem as bad as you sounded before you opened the door,' Jess said.

She was right. I'd forgotten to pile it on when she said she couldn't get in. 'Comes and goes,' I said, splurging onto the side of the bed nursing the mug and my scalded lips.

'You're very spotty,' she said then, checking out the face.

'Thanks.'

'Reaction to being with us maybe.'

'Yeah, that must be it. How was the last day?'

'Good. Nobody did any work.'

'Nothing new there then. The TV mob still about?'

'Yes, they're filming Mum answering questions about you being ill. Probably going to make a thing of it in the show.'

'I'm not talking to them about it,' I said.

'Better stay here then.'

She closed the door behind her. I sat there for a while blowing on the Bov and sipping carefully. Good as it was, it was my second liquid meal of the day and I felt a need for something solid. And here's a funny thing. When I thought of solids I thought of vegetables. Yep. Jiggy McCue had a fancy for a portion of veg. To tell you the truth I'm not sure how big a portion's meant to be. We're told to eat five portions of this or that a day, but if anyone's said what size a portion is I missed it. I'm guessing that it's quite important to know this. I mean how do I know that a portion of cauliflower isn't the whole thing? If it was, and we had to eat five whole cauliflowers a day, everyone would soon be the size of a block of flats – and maybe just a tad sick of cauliflower.

I also had a fancy for fruit. Fruit more than veg, in fact, probably because it's sweeter. But there was no fruit in the house. Or the garden. I was wondering vaguely where I could get some when Pete and Angie strolled into my mind. They could get me some, but I couldn't reach them to ask them on my mobile. To talk to them I had to get clear of the premises. Maybe I could sneak out and arrange to meet them once PP and Co had gone.

When Roo came up and knocked a bit later I scrambled under the duvet and told her to come in – not in my strongest voice, but not quite as feebly as the last time she saw me.

She looked round the door. 'How are you feeling now?'

'Bit better thanks.'

'Oh good. Dinner will be ready shortly.'

I noticed her eyes mooching around my spots, but she didn't say anything about them. I asked if it was OK if I stayed where I was.

'Stay here?'

'Yes. Rest. Recover properly.'

'Well, you can if you'd rather, of course you can. I'll ask Betty to bring something up for you.'

'Oh no, don't worry, I'll just get some sleep. How long are the crew gonna be here?'

'They're just packing up. Soon have the house to ourselves again.'

When she left I started to plan my getaway. To phone Pete and Angie I had to get beyond the grounds, but if I waited till it got dark they might not be allowed to come and meet me. Our parents are funny about us going out after dark. Nothing for it then. I had to risk being seen. In a while I watched the TV van drive away, followed by PP's car. I sighed when I saw Carla's flying hair in his passenger seat.

I took one last gander in the en-suite mirror before I went. The stripy toothpaste under my eyes had mostly flaked off by now, so I wiped the rest away. My five spots looked worse than ever and — oh, terrific! — a sort of rash had appeared on other parts of my phizog. I opened Mrs Moult's packet of custard powder and patted some on. The spots and rash immediately looked less red. I patted some more. Better still. Hey, maybe I'd discovered the perfect spot concealer. If I had money I could buy tons of custard powder, repackage it as 'McCue's Tried-and-Tested Bad Spot Cover', and make a fortune! If I made my fortune, I need never do what my parents or teachers said again. I could draw up outside the school or my house in my chauffeur-driven limo, wave briefly at everyone, and drive away, laughing. Who says money can't buy happiness?

Chapter Fourteen

After swapping my PJs and dressing gown for street clothes and pinning Carla's rosy gift to my jacket, I shoved the chair back under the door handle. Anyone who failed to move the door and couldn't get an answer to a yelled question would think I was asleep or wanted to be left alone. That was the hope anyway. If they didn't think that, if they kicked the door in and found me missing without even a row of pillows under the duvet pretending to be me, I might return to a squad of uniforms sitting on my bed with notepads and walkie-talkies. Had to take a chance on that.

When I was ready I opened the window and hoisted a leg over the ledge. This might not sound like a terrifically bright thing to do with Toby's room not being on the ground floor, but there was this big old tree right outside, and it had a thick bough that was just half a step off the ledge. I made it to the bough without any trouble, and as it was summer I was immediately hidden from roving eyes by a mass of leaves. I peered through the leaves and listened hard to make sure there was no one about, and when I was satisfied I inched along the bough and scrambled down the trunk on the side that faced away from the house. From there I hoofed it to the gates. The gates weren't closed, they never were, which made them pretty pointless in my opinion, but I was glad they were open right now.

Once off the premises I checked my phone. I had a signal! But rather than ring Pete and Angie so close to the house I set off for town. The town centre was about a fifteen minute hike and the road was quite open – only a few other houses along the way, and not much to hide behind – which made me feel quite vulnerable. I kept looking over my shoulder, and when cars zoomed towards me I pulled my head down into my jacket. It wasn't too likely that anyone on the road would know me, but as I was supposed to still be in my room I felt kind of like I shouldn't let my features be glimpsed even by strangers. I wondered if spies felt that way. Genuine spook-type spies, I mean. That could be why they wear false beards and hair and stuff wherever they...

Hey! A disguise! That's what *I* needed!

When I came to a phone box I went inside and called Angie on my mobile. Just as well I had the mobile, because the phone in the box had been smashed to pieces by the last user.

'Angie, it's me.'

'Who's me?' she said.

'Jiggy, who'd you think?'

'Jiggy. Hmm. Think I used to know someone of that name...'

'Stop messing about, Ange, I need your help.'

'Help? My help? Why would I help someone who doesn't keep in touch like he's been asked to?'

'I couldn't keep in touch. They put some sort of block on my phone so I couldn't ring you.'

'You're ringing me now.'

'That's 'cos I've snuck out. I'm on my way to town to meet you and Pete.'

'Meet us? But we're not in town, we're at home.'

'Yeah, well get your bums out of there and head townward. I need you to bring me some fruit and a disguise.'

'Some what and a what?'

'Fruit and a disguise.'

'This is a joke, right?'

'Joke? Why would it be a joke?'

'Well, because these are not normal things for a person to ring up and ask for.'

'Normal or not, they're what I need. The disguise is so no one will see my face. I don't trust that director. He could have cameras planted all over town to catch me if I sneak out. Which I have, so get moving.'

'Jig, I hadn't planned on going out tonight.'

'So replan. This is me here, not a casual acquaintance.'

'What do we tell Mum and Oliver?'

''Bout what?'

'About why we're going out, where we're going, who we're meeting. You know what they're like about us roaming the streets after tea.'

'Can't you tell 'em you're going to my house?'

'What, to see Toby?'

'Yeah, to see Toby. You have met him, haven't you?'

'Yes. Naturally. We were round there most of yesterday and today. And guess what. We're gonna be in the film too. They interviewed Pete and me as your best mates.'

'I hope you said nice things about me.'

'We told the truth.'

'And that means...?'

129

'We told the truth.'

'It better be a good truth,' I said. 'If you've trashed me on film I'll be advertising for new buds. Look, meet me at the shopping centre, soonest.'

'The shopping centre? The shops are shut.'

'I don't want to go shopping, I want to see you and Pete and put on the disguise you're gonna bring me.'

'What sort of disguise do you have in mind?'

'Not fussy. Anything that covers my face.'

She sighed. 'Well, all right. Where in the shopping centre?'

'Let's say the bogs in the square. Somewhere to sit and talk.'

'You want to talk on the public toilets?'

I ground my teeth. 'Outside them, Ange. Outside. OK?'

'OK. I'll get Pete. He probably won't be keen either. Ryan got him a pirate 18 cert death-and-destruction game today.'

'Ryan did? Since when was Garrett friendly with Ryan?'

'Since he said he can get any game he wants ultra cheap.'

'Well, tell the toe-rag I'll never forgive him if he doesn't come. Garrett, not Ryan.'

'If I tell him that he'll probably say he can live without your forgiveness.'

'Say it's a one for all, all for lunch situation. If that doesn't do it, tell him he's out of the Musketeers. And don't forget the fruit.'

'What is this fruit thing?'

'I have this craving.'

She laughed. 'Jiggy McCue craving fruit? Pull the one with bells on!'

'No, I mean it, I – '

'Save it,' she said, and hung up.

I took my time walking the rest of the way because I know from experience how hard it is to drag Pete away from one of his games. Because I had time to kill I read everything I passed that had words on it. Like the sign for the Rare Breed Visitor Centre, which made me wonder if you had to be a rare breed of visitor to get in, and the 'Plant Crossing' sign that got me imagining a huge shrub dragging its roots across the road. There were quite a few For Sale signs outside houses and I probably read every one, including the addresses and contact details of the estate agents who were trying to sell them. One of the houses had been sold by G Force & Son. The sign outside read: 'Sold by Force'. I liked that.

I also liked the big red-and-white notice in front of the church, though I'm not sure it was meant to be funny:

**DON'T LET WORRY
RUIN YOUR LIFE!
THAT'S WHAT THE
CHURCH IS FOR!**

One of the last streets before you get to the Brook Farm Shopping Centre from that side is Poplar Avenue. Now you'd expect a road called Poplar Avenue to be full of poplar trees, wouldn't you? Well it used to be. Poplar trees had lined both sides of that street since great-grandparents were throwing toys out of their prams, but a while back there were complaints from the bus company that the branches slapped the upper windows of the buses, so the council decided to get rid of the trees. Bad move. Not a 'poplar' decision. There were so many protests in the local rag that it looked as if the council would have to change its mind. But one dark night an army of very quiet tree surgeons moved in and turned every single poplar into a stump while the residents were asleep.

Since then someone had added a word to the sign at one end of Poplar Avenue. The word was 'No'. Now the sign read 'NO POPLAR AVENUE'.

Because all the shops were shut, the shopping centre was very quiet when I got there. Sometimes you get a few people without lives gazing into the windows of the closed shops, but tonight there was only one, a man in a hat and buttoned-up raincoat. The hat was one of those old-fashioned gangster-type ones. My dad had one just like it, though he never wore it. It was a warm evening, but the man had his collar turned up and his hat brim turned down, which made him look like someone up to no good, even though he was only mooching. I had a sudden suspicious thought. What if he was one of PP's people, one I didn't know, and he'd followed me from the house and had lost me and was trying to pick up my trail again? What if he had a little camera stashed in his raincoat to get some more film of me doing more stuff that would make me look bad? I backed sharply into a shop doorway, and stayed there till the man went round a corner. Then I tiptoed away, through the arcade to the little square where the public toilets are.

I parked myself on one of the benches by the raised flower-beds placed all round the square, and settled in to wait for P & A. Once I'd read all the names, messages and swear-words scratched into the bench my mind drifted back to another night the three of us had come to this spot. It was a couple of years earlier, the night we buried Aunt Hetty in the Ladies.* We were eleven then. Eleven! So much had happened to us since we were that age. Things that don't seem to happen to other kids. Mostly these things start with me. I have no idea why. All I want is a quiet life. Quiet life? My life spins from one disaster to another, and Pete and Angie almost always spin with me. Yes, the Three Musketeers had been through quite a lot together.

While I sat there, thinking these things, it started to rain. It wasn't a heavy rain. In fact it was kind of refreshing. I even tilted my face up and let it patter down on me for while. It didn't last long. Stopped just in time actually. Another minute and I'd have got pretty damn sick of it, I can tell you.

---

* Read all about it in *The Poltergoose*.

Chapter Fifteen

'There he is.'

Pete's voice. I looked sideways. He and Angie were coming out of the arcade. Pete had a carrier bag with him. Pete often has a carrier bag, usually with some junk in it, or some game with buttons he pushes all the time he's with us, which is very annoying for us if not for him.

'Took your time, didn't you?' I said.

'It was raining,' Angie said. 'We had to take cover.'

'Wimps. It wasn't much. And it's stopped now.'

'It's because it's stopped that we're here, and watch who you're calling a wimp, McCue.'

She flumped down beside me on the bench. Pete stayed on his feet, swinging his carrier bag at the flowers, knocking petals off.

'What's this all about then?' he asked.

'What it's all about is that I'm having a lousy time,' I said.

'From Toby's description of his gaff you've really

fallen on your feet,' Angie said. 'Horses, swimming pool, own bathroom. You don't know when you're well off.'

'It's the cameras. Every time I turn round there's a lens pointing at my jacksie.'

'Cameras here too.' She meant the CCTV cameras around the square, but they'd all been vandalised to death so they didn't count. 'You're never satisfied. Most people would kill for a chance to be on telly.'

'I'm not most people. Being on telly's the last thing I want.'

'The last thing?' Pete said, throwing himself onto the bench with us. 'My last thing would be a bubble bath in a vat of chocolate.'

We ignored him.

'What happened to your face?' Angie asked, looking at me properly for the first time.

'My face?'

'It's all yellow and streaky.'

'Uh?'

She took a little mirror out of her pocket and flashed it at me. I groaned. The light rain I'd enjoyed had turned the custard powder into actual custard and made it run. I yanked my hanky, spat on it, and scrubbed my face.

'Better?' I said when the job was done.

'Well, you're not yellow any more,' Angie said. 'But now you're covered in spots.'

'I'm not *covered* in spots. There's only five.'

'Seven,' she said, counting.

'Seven? No!'

I snatched her mirror and gaped at it. She was right. My five spots were now seven!

'What's it like living in the lap of luxury then, Jig?' Pete asked.

'Rather be at home,' I mumbled. Seven spots!

'Home? You're crazy. No swimming pool at home.'

'Who needs a swimming pool?'

'I wouldn't mind one. If I had a personal swimming pool I'd use it all the time.'

'No, you wouldn't.'

'I would.'

'You wouldn't. Two reasons. One, it'd be part of the scenery and not a novelty for long. Two, you don't like water.'

'That's washing water. Swimming pools are different. We've been to the local pool thousands of times.'

'Three,' I said.

'Three? I've been there more than that.'

'Maybe four. You always have excuses not to go when we want to.'

'That's because it's a public pool. A pool at home would be private. Different kettle of frogs altogether.'

'Well, the swimming pool *aside*,' I said, 'at home you know where you are. At home, where I *should* be, there's a terrific camera shortage.'

'Not now there isn't. Not in your home.'

'When the TV people aren't there, I mean. Then everything's all boring and normal the way I like it. No surprises.'

'No surprises!' Angie cried. 'Your life's nothing *but* surprises.'

'Oh, you don't understand!' I wailed.

'You're right, we don't.'

'Did you bring the fruit?'

'Fruit?'

'I asked you to bring some.'

'I thought you were kidding about that.'

'You mean you didn't?'

'No. Why would we? Jig, you never eat fruit.'

'I know, but right now I really fancy some.'

I was so disappointed about the fruit lack. I'd been looking forward to something fresh and fruity off the tree or bush ever since I phoned her.

'I suppose you didn't bring the disguise either.'

'Disguises are Pete's department,' Angie said.

Pete dipped into his carrier bag. When I saw what he took out of it I could only gasp.

'What's that?'

'The disguise.'

'When I asked for a disguise, I meant something that would make people not notice me. What are the chances of them not noticing a thirteen-year-old boy in horn-rimmed specs, big false nose and floppy moustache, all joined together?'

'Like I said, nothing's ever right for you,' Angie said. 'Toby's such a refreshing change from your moans and groans and problems.'

'She's right,' said Pete. 'Toby's terrific. We're thinking of making him an honorary Musketeer.'

'You're what?'

'Thinking of making Toby an honorary Musketeer.'

'You can't do that!'

'Why not?'

'Why not? Because there are three of us in the Musketeers. Three means three votes, and I haven't voted, and I wouldn't anyway because four into three won't go.'

'While you're away, there are only two Musketeers,' Angie said. 'So the remaining two can do what they like.'

'There's nothing in the rules about that,' I said.

'Exactly. So we can do it.'

I wasn't happy about this, but I hadn't met up with them to pick a fight, so I kicked the bench with my heels instead. I was still doing this when I caught a movement in the corner of one of my eyes.

'Hey, that man.'

The dodgy-looking type in the hat and raincoat had returned. He was strolling past the shopping centre end of the arcade, trying to pretend he hadn't seen us. But he had, I knew he had. I also knew for absolute certain now that he was following me for PP. It was just too much of a coincidence that someone in a pulled-down hat and an up-collared raincoat would appear the moment I did a runner, and keep on appearing.

I jumped to my feet. 'Let's go!'

I yanked my jacket over my head and hurried away, expecting P & A to follow. When I reached the corner of the square I looked back. They hadn't moved. I waved at them frantically. They looked at one another, then got up slowly and came after me, really taking their time until I jumped up and down a few times and did super-charged windmill impressions with my arms.

'What's going on?' Pete asked when they eventually joined me.

'That man,' I said.

'What man?'

'The one who's following me. Didn't you see him?'

'Saw an old geezer in a hat. I don't think he was following you.'

'Well take it from me, he was. Is. We have to get away from here.'

We were about to head off when I heard voices from around the next corner and went into one of the nervous jigs I can't help sometimes. I hastily slotted my features into the lousy disguise Garrett had brought. The people belonging to those voices could be more of PP's agents!

As it turned out, the couple who strolled round the corner arm-in-arm weren't interested in me at all. Didn't even notice me, in spite of the disguise. I kept it on anyway.

Chapter Sixteen

We didn't go far from the shopping centre, just walked round the outside of it. I soon got so used to the heavy glasses, big nose and moustache that I forgot they were there. We nattered as we walked, but even though we'd been incommunicoodo for days Pete and Angie didn't seem to care how things were going at the Next Family's. Even when I started telling them about Springhollow School they looked around like the view of absolutely nothing was more fascinating, so I pulled the plug on that topic too. They were much keener to tell me what it was like in our street with the TV squad there. They said the neighbours hung out of their windows all day, or stood in the street, or gurned or waved or walked behind anyone who was being filmed. Jolyon Atkins had mooned in his bedroom window when the camera panned along the street. Pete and Angie had met PP and like me they thought he was a creep. They said he kept putting his arm round my mother and whispering in her ear, and how she went all soppy and girly every time. They also went on and on about how great Toby was, and what a pity he didn't live on the estate full-time. I put up with this until we came to a certain high wall and gate and suddenly I had a good excuse to change the subject.

'Apples!' I cried, skidding to a halt.

'What?' said Angie.

The gate was one of those tall iron jobs, all fancy and black, with spikes like spears on top. I pointed through it, at the orchard beyond.

'In there. Millions of 'em. I'm going in. Coming?'

'In there?' said Pete. 'There could be someone watching.'

'What, like a Cox's Pippin Guardian? I don't think so.'

'Could be cameras.'

'Also unlikely. It's an orchard, not a bank.'

'We haven't scrumped apples since we were nine and got caught and grounded for a week.'

'Cluck-cluck,' I said through my fake moustache.

'I'm not chicken,' he said. 'It's just that – '

'I bet if your wonderful new pal asked you, you'd go, wouldn't you?'

'Toby?' said Angie. 'I can't see him *ever* suggesting nicking apples.'

'Look,' I said. 'I'm not talking about a massive heist here. We don't need to pick any locks, blow anything up, make sure the getaway bike's in gear. I just want to nip over the gate, grab an apple or two, and skedaddle. We'll be out again in less than two minutes.'

'Not worth all three of us going then, is it?' said Pete.

He had a point. 'No, guess not. Just thought... you know... one for all...'

'Well think again. We'll stand guard. Here.'

I sighed and started up the gate, a lone Musketeer in a false nose, glasses and moustache. What were things coming to when I had to do stuff on my own while my partners-in-crime since birth watched my backside rising solo into the sky?

'Mind those spikes up there,' Angie called softly. Suddenly we were speaking in hushed voices.

'Thanks,' I called softly back. 'Might not've thought of that if you hadn't mentioned it. Might have thrown myself on one of them and said "Oh dear" as it pierced my heart.'

'Forget I spoke,' she said.

'Did you?' I replied, still climbing.

As it turned out there was enough space between

the spikes for me to wriggle through without skewering something vital, and then I was scrambling down the other side. Well, clambering slowly. I don't do a lot of scrambling, even with eggs. The Climbing Wall on the common near the estate is a you-have-to-be-seriously-joking scenario for me.

I dropped down into the orchard and stood there for a sec. The nearest trees were just half a dozen metres away. No big deal to get to them and grab a pair of apples, but the open space between me and them made me a tad nervous.

'What are you waiting for?' Angie asked through the gate.

'I'm just getting my bearings.'

'You know your bearings. Your bearings are a private orchard. Get your rotten apples and – '

There was a reason why that sentence ended with 'and – '. The reason was the siren of a cop car. I jumped sideways and pressed myself against the wall so I couldn't be seen from the street, expecting the car to screech to a halt and half a dozen rozzers jump out, kick the gates in, cuff me, and drag me off to the cells to be interrogated under strong lights.

But the car went right on by, taking the siren with it.

I waited another sec or six before breathing again and calling out, super softly.

'Angie? Pete?'

No reply.

I looked through the gate.

'Angie?'

Nothing.

'Pete?'

A further nothing.

I pressed my moustache against the ironwork and peered out as well as I could with the big fake nose in the way. No sign of them. The Three Musketeers were down to One.

'Grrrrrr.'

That didn't come from me. It came from something behind me. I turned, slowly, as you do at such times. An enormous black hound was staring at me from where the trees started. His ears were pressed flat against his bony skull. His teeth were bared. Saliva dripped from his jaws. And he wasn't on a chain. My past life flashed before me in the time it takes to say 'Sod it.' *Now what?* I thought. Then I thought something else. The something else

147

was that maybe this would be a really terrific time to give up apples permanently.

I spun round. Grabbed gate. Hauled myself skyward like there was an Apollo rocket up me.

'GRRRRRRRAAAAAGH!'

The hound thumped the gate just below me and something powerful clamped one of my heels. I yanked my foot, got it free, shot further up the gate. Another thump as the beast tried to follow me, but he was a dog, he'd never done a gate-climbing course, and I was just beyond his reach, and scrambling – yes, scrambling! – like a madman.

When I got to the top, I slumped between a couple of spikes, half over the pavement on the street side, half not. On the orchard side, where my legs still were, the slavering apple minder chewed iron the way it would snack on bones if it caught me. This presented me with a new problem. As his front feet and jaws were pasted to the gate I couldn't climb down to the street, because when I reached the halfway point the McCue-hungry hound would be within a knuckle of me and in a couple of angry snaps I'd be armless, which is more than he was.

I had no choice but to jump.

Now jumping is another of those energetic things I try not to do too often. It's one of the many stupid activities that Mr Rice tries to get us to do in PE. Usually when the Ricipops tells us to jump up, down or along something, I think, 'What is the *point* of this?', but now I knew. It was so we'd be prepared to leap from tall gates when trying to escape wild beasts.

So I pulled the rest of me to the top of the gate, corrected the angle of my disguise, spread my arms, and sailed through the air like a feather with legs, well clear of the gate and the snarling beastie. It was a fine jump. What wasn't so fine was the landing. You know, I always imagined that if I ever needed to I could leap from tall buildings and when I got close to the ground I would bend my knees just so and land as gently as anything, then walk away with my hands in my pockets, whistling. But after the jump from the top of that gate maybe I won't try that, because one of my feet tilted as it landed, my leg gave way, and I thudded onto my side.

'Hey!'

That wasn't me. Wasn't the dog either. It was a man who wasn't on the scene last time I checked.

A man in a raincoat with the collar turned up and a hat brim over his eyes. While the insane mutt tried to force its head and body between the pattern of the gate and drown me in unfriendly saliva before toothing me to death, I lay scrunched on the ground in pain and the shady geezer I'd been running from stood over me. It was not one of the best positions I've ever been in.

I tried to get up and scoot, but my twisted foot wouldn't let me stand without holding on to the gate, so I gave it a miss.

'Get away from me!' I said to the man who'd been tracking me. I knew that any minute he would pull out a camera and start filming, if he wasn't already from between the buttons of his coat.

'Jig?'

I frowned behind my horn-rims. I knew that voice. And when the man raised the brim of his hat, I saw why.

'Dad!'

'Shut it, you!'

This wasn't to me, it was to the beast trying to get at us through the gate. The dog didn't shut it, so Dad kicked the gate. The dog snarled back at him, so he kicked the gate harder. The dog stopped snarling, but he didn't leave, just stood there growling at us through the pretty pattern.

'What were you doing up there?' Dad said, turning back to me. 'And why are you wearing that?'

'Wearing what?' He tapped the end of my false nose. 'Oh, this. I was trying a new look.'

I slipped the disguise over my head and tossed it high in the air. It went over the gate. The dog leapt for it, grabbed it in its jaws, and set about tearing glasses from nose from moustache.

'Gimme a hand, willya?' I said to my father. 'Think I twisted my ankle.'

He leant down and helped me up. I winced. When I was on both feet I leant on his arm. He asked me again what was going on.

'I wanted an apple,' I told him.

'Well take my advice,' he said. 'Next time run a check on the mad dog situation first.'

'I'll try and remember that. What's with the hat and coat?'

'I needed a break from those TV people.'

'You're a grown man,' I reminded him. 'Couldn't you have just strolled out looking normal?'

'What, and have them catch me on camera and make something of it in the commentary?

No, I thought it best to sneak out the back way.'

'And keep your head down, even away from the house?'

'Seemed wise. I never know where they'll pop up next.' He sighed. 'Every time I shove a hand down my pants or a finger up my nose, I find they've filmed me through a vase of flowers or something. It's as if DD's going out of his way to make me look bad.'

Sounds familiar, I thought. 'How do you get on with him?' I said.

'DD? Oh, you know…'

'No. Tell me.'

'Well, since you ask, I want to punch him senseless every time he enters a room.'

'And Mum?'

'No, I don't want to punch her.'

'I mean what does she think of him?'

'Oh, she thinks he's the cat's whiskers. Well, she would. He's all over her. Soft-soaping her the whole time, paying her compliments. She loves it.'

'Maybe you ought to have a word with him.'

'I'd like to have two,' Dad said. 'But I have to be careful. Upset him and he could make me look even worse in his lousy film. What's that?'

He touched the little rose pin on my coat.

'Carla gave it to me.'

His eyes glazed over. 'Ah, Carla...'

'Nice, isn't she,' I said.

'Mmmm.' He said it like he'd just licked his favourite icecream.

'How's the swap side of things going?'

'Sorry?' His mind was still on Carla.

'The swap. Having Toby there instead of me.'

'Oh, *that's* going well, if nothing else is. Good lad, young Toby.'

'So I hear.'

'Good-natured, goes along with everything, fits in a treat.'

'OK, I get it. Sounds like you got a terrific deal landing him.'

'Yeah. Be sorry to part with him.'

'How does PP treat him?'

'PP?'

'DD. My name for him. Does he keep catching Toby in embarrassing situations?'

'Not that I know of. I don't think Toby does anything embarrassing.'

'No, he wouldn't. Listen, I'd better get back.'

'Yeah, me too.'

We turned to head for the shopping centre, from where we would head off in different directions. We didn't get far before a voice rang out from a car with dark windows parked across the road.

'Thanks, chaps!'

One of the rear windows of the car was a quarter down and a camera lens was in the gap, but the voice hadn't come from the gap. It had come from the face in the front passenger seat. PP's face. I just gaped. So did Dad. What was he doing here? And not in his usual car either. And then we got it. It was a spy car.

'How long have you been here?' demanded my father, crossing the road. I limped painfully after him.

PP smirked. 'Long enough to get some fine footage of Jimmy in a jokey disguise making a swift exit from private property pursued by a guard dog, and of you looking like something out of a bad detective movie. You know, Mel, according to your contract, you're not to meet with your son till the filming's over. It's not going to look good in the episode.'

'How did you know we were here?' I asked him.

PP tapped the side of his nose. 'Be surprised what I know.'

He was laughing as he wound his window up and the car zoomed away. Dad and I watched it go. Then we looked at one another. There was nothing to say. I don't know what he was thinking, but I know what I was. That we were going to be royally stitched up for the amusement of millions of viewers, and there wasn't a thing we could do about it.

Chapter Seventeen

It was the night after the night of the orchard incident. I was lying in bed watching something on Toby's TV that I wouldn't be allowed to watch at home when there was a little knock on the window. Now like I said before, that window was not on the ground floor, so if someone was out there they must have either climbed the tree or been a bird beaking the glass. The curtains were drawn so I couldn't see who or what had done the tapping, which made me kind of uneasy. By kind of uneasy I mean sick with terror. I pulled the duvet up to my chin and turned the telly down with the remote.

'Is there anybody there?'

That was me.

'...... .....'

That was the answer.

But the little knock came again, so I gave it another shot.

'Is there anybody *out* there?'

'...... .....'

Same answer. Whoever it was, if it was a person, he didn't seem to be in a very chatty mood. But then I heard a whistle. It wasn't a long whistle, or a loud one, not one of those finger-and-thumb-in-the-mouth jobs that I can't do, but it was quite tuneful, which made me think it must be a bird after all.

I let go of the duvet, slid out of bed, went to the window. I knew the window was open a little bit because I'd left it that way before drawing the curtains and getting into bed. A bird could probably squeeze in if it beaked the curtains, but I didn't want a bird flapping round the room. If I yanked the curtains back suddenly it would panic and fly away, I thought. So I gripped the curtains, one in each hand, and jerked, one one way, the other the other.

And screamed silently.

The silent scream was for what I found sitting on the bough of the tree that almost reached the window.

'About time,' said the person on the bough. 'One more tap and whistle and I was jacking it in. You think I have nothing better to do than sit out here waiting for you to come to the window?'

'Who … who … who…?' I said.

'Yeah, terrific owl impression, but can I come in? You have to invite me or I can't enter, like you do with vampires.'

'Vam … vampires?'

'I said *like* you do with vampires, not that I was one. Do I *look* like a vampire?'

What he looked like was this. He was ultra-thin and he had these really bony wrists and long fingers with long nails, and he wore pointed shoes, and this dull greeny-grey suit sort of thing. On his head he wore a matching floppy hat with a tassel that kept swinging in front of his eyes and which he kept brushing away, and his face was all wrinkled, like he'd been a heavy smoker for fifty years. I was still wondering what he was supposed to be if not a vampire when he told me.

'I'm an elf,' he said.

'A what?' I said.

'An elf. The very elf that's going to offer you the kind of life other kids only dream about.'

'What do you mean – elf?'

'I *mean*,' he said, 'that that's what I am. Now are you going to invite me in or are you not going to invite me in? If not, fine, I'll be on my way to the next lucky kid on my list.'

'List?'

'Invite me in and I'll explain everything.'

'I can't invite you in just like that,' I said. 'I mean, here you are, in a tree outside my window, telling me you're an elf with some kind of offer. Does that really sound like the sort of thing anyone who hasn't had a lobotomy recently would fall for?'

He sighed. 'Every now and then I meet a kid who won't take my word for it, and you're obviously the latest. I'm guessing you never met an elf before.'

'You're guessing right. And why would I believe I'm meeting one now?'

'You want proof, is that it?'

'Proof would be good.'

He batted his swinging tassel away again and lifted one side of his floppy hat. Underneath, as you might expect, was an ear. But what an ear! It was pointed at the top. Very pointed. I stared for a few seconds, but then curled the McCue lip. I'm not a mother. I'm not so easily fooled.

'You probably bought that and its chum on the other side from Zappa's Joke Shop in town.'

The tree-squatter covered his pointy lug and leaned towards the window. 'My ears are as real as yours, Sunny Jim, only prettier.'

'Sunny Jig,' I said.

'What?' he said.

'Never mind.'

'Look, tell you what. You raise the window and I'll let you feel my ears to see how real they are. How's that? I don't do that for every spoilt brat in town.'

'Oh sure,' I said. 'I open the window to feel your ears, you leap in, beat me to a pulp, and burgle the house.'

He came over all shocked-looking at this. 'Burgle the house? I'm no burglar. I don't beat kids up either, even though it sometimes seems like a pretty neat way of passing the time. Burgling and beating people up are not part of Elvish culture.'

I frowned – and didn't shut the window like most people would. Most people wouldn't give such twaddle the time of day, but I'd run into some pretty wild characters in my life, and how did I know this wasn't another? The weirdo on the bough must have realised he was close to convincing me because he slipped a wallet out of his rumpled old jacket and took out a small card, which he put against the glass for me to see.

'My ID,' he said. 'And I don't show this to everyone either.'

'It's a drawing,' I said.

'So?'

'A photo might seem more authentic.'

'Elves don't use cameras,' he said. 'Human technology's not for us.'

'It's not even a very good drawing.'

'What do you mean, not good? It was done by an official elf artist.'

'El fartist?'

'Elf. Artist. You could do with ears like mine, you'd hear better.'

'Maybe your artist should be looking for other kinds of work,' I said. 'Drain clearance, say. It doesn't look like anything like you.'

'I was quite a bit younger when this was drawn,' he said.

'Before you went to seed, eh?'

'Hey, are you this rude to every elf that comes calling or are you just trying it out on me? It's an official likeness. As in Official Likeness. Look at the stamp.'

In the corner of the drawing was a tiny round stamp with three capital letters followed by four numbers.

I felt my lips twitch. 'Tit?' I said.

'What?'

'That's what it says on the stamp. TIT 7509.'

'The number is the elvish year the drawing was made,' said the anorexic in the ancient suit. 'The letters stand for *Teriolanus Incustiba Transo* – Elvish for "Year of the Great Elf".'

'Great Elf?'

'The first of our kind to learn to write his name with his tongue behind his teeth. Our calendar dates from the year of his execution by goblins.'

I laughed. 'First elves, then goblins? What next, fairies?'

He spat at the tree. 'Don't talk to me about those conniving little scumbags. Only good one I ever saw was stuffed, on a mantelpiece. Made my day.'

I took another decko at the ID card. There were two words printed under the bad drawing.

'Is that your name?'

'Of course it's my name. Why would anybody else's name be with my picture?'

'Well, as the picture doesn't look like you, the

name could be somebody else's too. Some name. Regis Affa... what is it?'

'Regis Affalonious. Junior actually. It was my dad's name before me.'

'And he passed it on to you? Sounds like elf abuse to me.'

He shoved the card angrily back in his jacket.

'You're supposed to be a likeable kid,' he said. 'That's what it says on the docket. Unless...'

'Unless what?'

'Unless I've come to the wrong window and you're not Toby Next.'

'Toby Next?'

He leaned forward, peered into my face.

'You are him, aren't you?'

'Don't you know?' I said. 'Don't you have a bad drawing of him too?'

'Him. You said him. So you're not Toby Next.'

'That depends.'

'Depends? On what?'

'On what you want. What makes you think I'm Toby anyway?'

'Until now I had no doubt,' he said. 'I have very precise directions to this window. Unless Toby's moved to another room since I received my instructions, this is where he sleeps.'

'What do you want with him?' I asked.

'That's for his unpointed ears alone.'

'But they might be my unpointed ears.'

'I think it's my turn to ask for proof of that,' the person on the bough said.

'Would it be a good thing for me to be Toby Next?'

'The best. You'd have it made. For life.'

Now I could have told him the truth and got rid of him right then and there, but if I did that I wouldn't learn what this was all about, and if I didn't learn what it was about I could be wondering about it till the day they sprinkle me over the roses. So I looked around the room for some way to convince him that I was who he thought I was before this insane conversation started. My eyes locked on the Good Luck card face down on the chest of drawers. I went over to it, brought it back to the window, slapped it against the glass with the message facing out.

'"Good luck, Toby"?' the maybe-elf read. 'Luck with what?'

'Exams,' I said, flipping the card back towards the

chest of drawers. It fell short, onto the floor. 'Now what's this all about?'

'You have to let me in first,' he said.

'Mm, well, still not so sure about that.'

'Well either get sure or say goodnight. I haven't got forever, and this tree is not well upholstered.'

'Don't go away.'

I drew the curtains across the window, shutting him out.

'What are you doing?' his voice said from the other side.

'Thinking. Gimme a minute.'

My thought was that even if he really was an elf I couldn't let him in just like that. He might be old and scrawny, but how did I know he wasn't a blue belt in elf karate or something? I needed to be ready to defend myself just in case. I looked around for a weapon. Saw nothing weaponish. Even the book Toby had left on the bedside table was only a paperback. I went to the en-suite and looked in.

'How long's this minute gonna take?' a muffled voice asked from the bough.

'About sixty seconds,' I said.

At first I didn't see anything in the en-suite

either, but then I did, and I whipped it out of its holder, went back to the window. I opened the curtains.

'What's that for?' the elf said, eyeing the dripping thing in my hand.

'For you if you get violent.'

'It's a lavatory brush.'

'It's all I could find at short notice.'

'Not very trusting, are you?'

'My mother told me never to talk to strange elves.'

I yanked the window a bit higher. (It was one of those sash windows that go up and down.) The elf stuck his head in, then wriggled the rest of him after it and landed on his hands on the carpet. Then he did a sort of back-flip and stood up. At full stretch the top of his head was about level with my chest.

'You're not a very *big* elf,' I said.

He scowled. 'We can't all be Orlando Bloom. Do you ever get past the insults, or are you just warming up?'

'Look,' I said. 'I've proved that I'm Toby Next. Now what do you want with him? Me?'

'I'm here to offer you a free ticket to a great life.'

'Free ticket? Great life?'

He dug in his jacket again and came up with a crumpled strip of yellow paper.

'Accept this and you'll be lucky in everything you do. You'll get some great girlfriends, go to one of the best universities, graduate in a blaze of glory, get a top job, hitch up with a rich and beautiful woman, be sickeningly happy, have three cheerful, high-achieving kids, and live to see your ninety-eighth birthday in perfect health.'

'And to get all that I'd have to do … what?'

'Why do you think you have to do something?'

'There's gotta be a catch. My dad says nothing good ever comes for free.'

'He's wrong, kid. You won life's lottery, is all.'

'Did I enter it?'

'You entered it the day you were born. All births are registered in the Great Elvish Scrolls, the bornéd are monitored by High Command, and those few who tick all the boxes by the time they're thirteen are visited by Life-Lot Elves such as myself, who then make the offer I'm making now.'

'And Toby Next ticks all the boxes, does he?'

The elf cocked his head and looked at me suspiciously. 'You're still saying the name like it's not yours.'

'It's a thing I do. I'm Toby Next. You've seen the proof.'

I pointed at the Good Luck card on the floor.

'All right,' he said. 'But I have to ask the Question. Give you the Vital Choice.'

'And what's that?'

'This. Do you, Toby Next, want the terrific life I just mentioned?'

'Are you sure I wouldn't have to do anything to get it? Like, you know, sell my soul to a devil or something?'

'You don't have to sell a thing. All you got to do is snatch my hand off, say "Close the window on your way out", and life's your oyster till you're even older than me.'

'These boxes Toby ticked. I mean that I ticked. What were they?'

He clicked his tongue. 'You're not making this easy, are you?'

'It's a big decision.'

He whipped out a small computer pad and started to scroll through what was on it. It looked pretty much like human technology to me, but I kept this to myself.

'The boxes you ticked are as follows. Cheerful,

optimistic, outgoing? Yes. Come from a good home? Yes. Parentage? Dad's a top surgeon. Do well at school? Yes. Good at sports? Yes. Show every sign of being successful in anything you attempt? Yes. Possess qualities that mark you out as a winner? Yes. Attractive?' He looked up, at my face. 'Well, that's one they got wrong. But anyway, you get the idea.'

'So does it mean that if I wasn't that sort of person I wouldn't be offered a perfect future?'

He put his pad away. 'Right.'

'Like, for instance, if I lived on the Brook Farm Estate and had parents who have a rust-bucket car and fight all the time, a dad who's out of work, an alley cat for a pet, and I only did so-so at school, was always in trouble for answering back, and was really lousy at sports...'

'Wouldn't get a look-in,' the elf said. 'High Command has better things to do than give a leg up to any old riffraff.'

'You look like you could do with a good-life ticket yourself,' I said.

He squinted at me. 'You being personal again?'

'I just meant that maybe you could do with some better clothes.'

'This is a traditional elvish suit.'

'Looks like the elvish left the building quite a while ago.'

'I've had it from new. Forty-two years. I was just starting out when it was assigned to me. The suit comes with the job, see.'

'And the food? That come with it too?'

'The food?'

'You look as if you don't eat.'

'I'm just small-boned. Can we move on here? My offer? The free ticket to a great life?'

'What if I turn it down?'

'Why would you, when there are absolutely no strings and it won't cost you a thing, even your mingy soul?'

'I'm just asking. What would happen to me if I said thanks but no thanks?'

He shrugged. 'Who knows? Who'd care? You'd be just another poor sap stumbling across the scrapheap of life. Most of what happens to you if you decline my generous offer will be down to luck. It doesn't say anything about your luck on your chart. How is it, scale of one to ten?'

'About three.'

'I wouldn't count on much going your way then.

Now do you want the ticket or don't you?'

'You're absolutely sure you couldn't give it to a kid like the one I mentioned? He's a real boy, by the way. Name of Jiggy McCue.'

The elf shook his head. 'Life tickets aren't transferable.'

'OK then.'

'You accept the wonderful future I'm offering?'

'No. Stuff it.'

His mouth dropped open. 'Uh?'

I snatched the yellow ticket off him, tore it in two, dropped the halves. As they headed for the carpet they dissolved in two sparkly puffs. The elf stared in amazement at the space where the ticket no longer was. Then he stared up at me.

'Why would you refuse a successful, wealthy, happy, trouble-free life?'

'I'm funny that way. Ni-night.'

I pointed at the window. The elf went to the ledge and climbed out. I closed the window behind him, drew the curtains, and smiled. Toby Next could take his chances along with the rest of us.

Chapter Eighteen

After Hector my rabbit was served up to me at dinner, I tried to stop wondering what was on my plate at the Next Family's and just swallowed. It helped that most of it was quite tasty. I was even getting used to the lunchtime pills and laxative. My spots were getting worse, though. Much worse. Daily. Some of the bigger ones were kind of oily-looking, with heads. If they carried on growing that way my face would soon be thick with heads. I just hoped they wouldn't look like someone I didn't want to be reminded of every time I looked in the mirror. Eejit Atkins, say. Or Mr Rice.

'Something wrong, Jiggy?'

Roo. Who'd come across me sitting in a shadow while PP and Co were filming something else.

'Wrong? No.'

'Come on, you can tell me.'

I puffed my cheeks out. 'It's these spots. There are more of them every day. Hate to think what they'll look like on screen.'

'I have something that might help,' Roo said. 'I would have mentioned it before, but I didn't like to in case it was a touchy subject.'

'It is a touchy subject. But I'll try anything.'

'Wait there.'

She went upstairs and when she came down again she had this jar of pale green cream.

'What is it?' I asked.

'Extract of rhinoceros testicle.'

'Pardon?'

'It's supposed to ease pains in joints, but I've found that it reduces all sorts of swellings too.'

'Including spots?'

'And boils. Toby gets them sometimes. Works a treat on him.'

So I let her put some of the rhino-testicle cream on my spots. I didn't ask her to, she offered, and she didn't shudder every time she touched a festering growth, which I thought was nice of her. The cream smelt like Bryan Ryan's armpits after football, but I could live with that if it meant that I would soon be spot-free.

While she was with me Roo told me about this big-deal event the family was taking part in on Saturday. A Sans-earthist jamboree.

'What's that?' I said.

She explained. 'There are four jamborees every year in different parts of the country. This one's our region's. There'll be speeches, music, dancing – and lots of our food, naturally.'

'Many people there?'

'Should be. Sans-earthism is spreading as a lifestyle choice, and after this weekend millions more will know about it.'

'How come?'

She smiled. 'Have you forgotten that we have a TV crew practically living with us?'

'Wish I had.'

'Knowing the jamboree would take place while they were filming was our prime motive for participating in Kid Swap. Our episode will give us the kind of exposure you can't usually get for love or money.'

'So they'll be there too,' I said with a sinking heart.

'Oh yes. DD's very keen.'

'He would be.'

There was more filming at the house before Saturday, but not a huge amount. When PP wanted sound-bites and didn't think it worth him coming over himself he gave Jack questions to ask us and film us answering them. I wasn't sorry to see less of PP, but I missed Carla, who was only there when he was. (When they did come it was always in his sporty car, never the sly one he'd used to catch Dad and me meeting at the orchard.)

When Saturday dawned the Next Family was all buzzy, even Jess, who told me she enjoyed their jamborees. They put on special purple and yellow T-shirts with some quote on the front about 'the tainted earth'. They gave me Toby's to wear.

The jamboree was set to occur at the showground on the edge of town. Most of our big outdoor events happen there. Things like fairs, circuses, fêtes and stuff. It was another warm day, very bright, and there were all these purple and yellow Sans-earthist banners on tall poles, and others as well as us in the T-shirts, though a lot more wore ordinary clothes. Solomon said that most of the folk in civvies were non-Sans-earthists who would go anywhere for a plate of free grub. There was plenty of that there, on long trestle tables. I had no idea what three-quarters of the food was except that no part of it had started out in the ground, but looking at it all laid out like that I found myself almost longing for a mouthful of veg. This was a pretty boggling almost-longing for someone who'd always believed that vegetables were created by wicked mothers to make their kids' lives a misery.

'Glad to see you're still wearing it!'

I looked up from the food tables. Carla.

She touched the little rose pin on my chest.

'Oh,' I said. 'Yes.'

I glanced over her gorgeous brown shoulder (it was bare today) and saw the TV van pulling up behind her boss's car. PP was leaning over the bonnet of the car, polishing a bit that the sun must be missing. He was dressed differently today, in a brown check jacket and flat cap, like this was a car rally or he was on holiday or something. Berk.

'That man and his car,' Carla said. 'He can't stand the slightest speck of dirt on it, inside or out. When I'm a passenger I have to be careful what I touch in case I leave a fingermark. If another vehicle ever backed into it, I reckon he'd fall on his face, bawling his eyes out.'

She laughed (terrific laugh), and I laughed too. It felt good, the two of us laughing at a joke nobody else was in on. Unfortunately PP must have heard us because he waved us over. Except when we got there...

'I was calling Carla,' he said to me, 'but as you're here, Jim, let's make the most of a day away from the house, shall we? We can show you mingling, sampling the food, twitching to the music and so on – OK?'

'Depends what the "so on" is,' I said suspiciously.

He flashed one of his pearly-white grins. 'What do you say we play it by ear?'

I knew what that meant. It meant that he and Jack would be on the lookout for me doing something that would give the viewers even more laughs at my expense. I clenched my jaw. Not today. Today they were going to be disappointed.

'Run along and play now, though, will you?' PP said then. 'I'll let you know when I need you. 'Kay?'

I didn't like being told to run along and play, especially by him, but I shrugged like it was all the same to me, nodded at Carla, and wandered off. Her boss and I were definitely not on course to become blood-brothers any time soon.

As I'd never heard of Sans-earthism until I moved in with the Next Family, I thought there were probably only a few of their lot, but cars and camper vans were arriving all the time with people in purple and yellow T-shirts. When they met other Sans-earthists they hugged if they were women or girls and shook hands if they were men or boys. I even saw little boys of about five shaking hands. But they weren't a serious lot. It didn't feel like a religion or anything, and there was lots of laughter. It felt like some club people had joined and really liked being members of, even the little ones, who would go off and run around together even if they'd never met before. Kind of sweet really.

Now it might not surprise you to hear that jamboree-type-things aren't my sort of deal. I was only there because I had to be. But I didn't feel too out of it because the Next Family made sure I wasn't on my own too much. If all three of them couldn't be with me they tried to make sure that one of them was. I even spent some solo time with Solomon for the first time when he asked me to help him set up some speakers on a little stage where a bunch of musicians were getting themselves and their instruments together. While we were seeing to the speakers Solomon told me stuff about Sans-earthism that I didn't need to know, such as that it was started by this Californian rock star in the 1970s, and that there were hundreds of thousands of followers now, in all corners of the world.* I didn't listen to much of what he said, just nodded and mumbled 'Mm' and 'Oh yeah?' when it seemed right to say such things.

Solomon was one of the speakers when the speeches started, but I didn't listen too hard to him then either. Or the rest of the speeches. They were all about Sans-earthism and how 'right' it was not to eat stuff that comes from the ground. My mum wouldn't have agreed with that. Nor would about six billion vegetarians. Jack filmed Solomon doing his bit, but didn't bother with the other speakers. The speeches were followed by amateur entertainment. One of the acts was a bunch of little kids in the T-shirts singing a Sans-earthist song accompanied by a man on a piano keyboard. The crowd cheered them like they were stars, which they definitely weren't. Jack filmed the kids and the audience, plus people chatting and laughing all around the field. Every so often he aimed his camera at me. I'd got used to this after a week of it and had no trouble carrying on like I didn't know I was being filmed, except that I made *absolutely sure* not to do anything that would make me look bad.

I spent most of the time with Jess, but sometimes

---

* I've often wondered about that. How many corners can a round world have...?

she had to go and say hello to friends, and then I felt kind of solitary, standing there trying to look like I belonged as much as the T-shirt I was wearing. One of these times that I was on my own – Jess and her mum were welcoming some dancers who'd just arrived in a trailer – Carla strolled over and asked how I was enjoying the day.

'I could think of other things I'd rather be doing,' I said.

'So could I,' she said. 'But it's not so bad, is it?'

'No, not so bad, but…'

She looked at me. 'Yes. Know what you mean.'

When she said this she half smiled and sort of fluttered her eyes in a way that I'd seen gorgeous female types half smile and flutter on big and small screens so many times. On screens. No one had ever looked at *me* that way before. My heart almost jerked out of its socket and hit her in the face. She was telling me that she liked me. I mean, *really* liked me. In spite of all my spots.

Chapter Nineteen

I was still rolling my eyes at the thought that Carla liked me when Jess returned. 'Problem,' she said. 'The dancers are one short. There have to be eight, but Janine just phoned to say her car's broken down on a roundabout miles away. The Sans-earthist dance sequence is the jamboree finale. Without it the day will just peter out – and with the cameras here too!'

'Oh, pity,' Carla said. 'I love watching dancers.'

'You'd probably have enjoyed our troupe then. They're pretty unusual.'

'What sort of dancing is it?'

'It's sort of a cross between clog dancing and jiving, and then some.' Jess looked sadly around. 'A lot of people are going to be very disappointed when they hear.'

'Isn't there anyone who can stand in for Janice?'

'Janine. No. The Sans-earthist finale is the group's speciality. The moves and steps need to be well practised.'

'I'm quite quick at picking up dance moves...' Carla said.

Jess looked at her. 'It's a complicated dance. You can't step into someone's clogs just like that.'

'Why don't I have a word with them and see?'

'Well, you could have a *word*, but – '

Carla was already on her way to where the seven dancers were standing. The blokes wore purple flared trousers and puffy-sleeved yellow shirts. The gals wore yellow sweaters and swirly purple skirts. They all wore wooden clogs. Yellow with purple toe-caps. Brightly as they were dressed, they looked really cheesed off. When Carla joined them and asked her question they shook their heads. She asked another question. One of the females did some moves with her hands and feet. Jess was right. It was complicated. But when Carla copied the moves perfectly the dancers raised their eyebrows at one another. Then one of the male dancers (who looked too old and heavy to be dancing *anything*) threw his arms in the air and flipped twice one way and once the other while doing some mad clog chopping down below – and Carla copied all this too, totally, without one wrong move. Again the dancers did the eyebrow thing. Now a third dancer jumped in the air, made some rapid elbow stabs, and jerked his knees this way and that, ending with a fancy clog shuffle. And Carla did the same thing *exactly*!

'She didn't lie,' Jess said to me.

'About what?'

'Being quick at picking up dance moves.'

The dancers were impressed too. One of the females went into the trailer and came back with Janine's costume. Jess told me that Janine was the only one who didn't travel with the troupe but they always carried her costume with theirs. The dancer held the sweater and skirt against Carla. They looked to be just her size. Carla tried on Janine's clogs and they fitted too. To prove it, she did something insane with her cloggy feet. The three females hugged her. The four men just beamed.

'Looks like she's saved the day,' Jess said.

'Mm,' I murmured. 'Good old Carla.'

She gave me a look that said she knew what Carla did to me. I felt my spot-loaded face heat up.

But before Carla could join the dance troupe for the day she had to get the go-ahead from PP, who was back at his car telling some kids off for leaning on it. When she reached him there was a bit of chat, then he called Jack over and had a conflab with him.

Jack nodded, and he and Boz started moving their gear to the dance platform that had been set up in front of the stage. While PP arranged ropes round his precious car to stop people getting too close, Carla went back to the dancers, grinning hugely. She'd got the OK and was going to be filmed in action. Now this I had to see! I moved closer to the platform. Jess came with me.

The dancers made some air sketches of the movements Carla would have to do. Then she went into the trailer to change into Janice's outfit. While she was in there, visitors and Sans-earthists started heading our way from all over the field. Word must have got about that the dancing would start any time.

When Carla came out of the trailer in Janice's costume, a secret sigh escaped me. She looked fantastic, even in the clogs, and so happy, like she couldn't wait to start dancing. She and the others got into position, the four men facing the four women. When they were all set to go, the band struck up the first dance tune – a weird mix of rock and brass-band, with a fiddle in there somewhere, kind of mad, but very lively. When the dancing started, Carla didn't get the first few moves absolutely right, but she soon got the hang of it and hardly put a clog wrong after that. I was quite proud of her, if you want to know.

Once the dancers really got going it was impossible not to move your feet and arms as well. Hard for me anyway. Others in the crowd were just tapping their feet or clapping out of rhythm, but me, after half a minute, I was really into it.

'Now I know why you're *really* called Jiggy!' Jess shouted over the music.

'What do you mean?' I bawled back.

'You're dancing just like them!'

'I'm not!'

'You are!'

I checked my arms and legs. She was right. I'd picked up the dance moves without noticing. I pulled my hands out of the sky and forced my feet to keep still. It wasn't easy. They wanted to keep going.

'Oh, don't stop!' Jess yelled.

'I hate dancing!' I replied.

'But you're so good!'

'Me? Nah!'

'You! Yah!'

As I was trying to make myself stand still,

I remembered something a teacher said to me a while back. That I was a natural dancer. Well, she *thought* she meant me, but she was actually talking about a boy who looked like me in every way apart from the ear department.* The one other thing that was different about him and me was that he didn't have the jigginess that gave me my name. But here was a thought. If he was like me in every other way and he danced really well, could it be that I could also dance if I wanted to? I wasn't sure I liked the sound of that. If the news ever got back to Ranting Lane that I was another Billy Elliot, I would be a laughing stock. Some of the boys would spray-paint the info all over town.

I was still thinking this when I caught Carla and a couple of the other dancers looking my way and laughing. What's so funny? I wondered. Then I realised. My body had joined in the dance again while my mind was on other things. My hands, arms, feet, everything, were moving just the way the dancers' hands, arms, feet and everything were. I couldn't believe it. I always said that I'd rather stand on my head in a bucket of hippo dung than dance in public. All right, I sometimes called my jiggy movements dancing, but that was

---

* See the ninth Jiggy book: *The Iron, the Switch and the Broom Cupboard.*

only because they *reminded* me of dancing. Now, though, in this crowded place, I wasn't just twitching or flapping or doing one of my agitated quick-steps. I was kicking my knees and feet up, swaying this way and that, spinning half round, half back, and flinging my arms about so nearby people had to duck or lean away. When I realised that I was copying the Sans-earthist dancers, I felt quite self-conscious at first, but when the crowd started cheering me as much as Carla and the actual dancers, I got over it and just … well, carried on.

By the end of the second dance – I danced along with that one too (couldn't help myself) – one of the men on the platform looked like he was having trouble keeping up. He was the one I'd thought seemed a bit old and heavy for such a hectic routine. When the dance ended he was really out of breath and red in the face. This was probably the reason one of the others announced that they would take a short break. Then they all went into a huddle.

'Jiggy!' Jess said. 'Where did you learn Sans-earthist dancing?'

I frowned. 'Nowhere.'

'Well you can't have just picked it up in a minute, watching them.'

'Carla did.'

'Yes, but she loves dancing. You said you hate it.'

'I do.'

'It doesn't look like it.'

'No, it doesn't,' said a voice behind me.

It was one of the male dancers. One of the female ones was with him. So was Carla.

'You put on quite a show there,' said the lady dancer.

'Sorry,' I said. 'I'll move away when you start again.'

'Move away? We're hoping you'll join us.'

'Join you?'

'Leonard's a bit puffed. He's been told by his doctor not to over-exert himself, and we think it would be a bit risky for him to carry on.'

'We thought you might take his place for the rest of the dances,' said the female dancer.

'Take his place?' I said. 'You mean dance up there with you?'

'Precisely,' the male dancer said.

'I couldn't,' I said. 'I'd be… embarrassed.'

'Didn't seem very embarrassed just now,' the lady dancer said.

'Well no, but…'

It was true. Once I'd got used to people's eyes on me I'd just got on with the dancing. But that didn't mean I –

Carla and the others were already walking me towards the platform.

'Now wait a minute...' I said.

They didn't wait. They kept on going, and so did I.

While we'd been talking, Leonard – the dancer who'd dropped out for health reasons – had been to the trailer and changed out of his yellow shirt with puffed sleeves. I was still trying to argue my way out of joining the troupe when he handed them to me, along with his clogs. In a sort of daze, I slipped my feet into the clogs. They felt like wooden canoes. There was enough room in each of them for twenty toes.

'Too big,' I said, thinking this would get me out of it.

No chance. One of the female dancers fell to her knees, whipped the clogs off, rammed some scrunched-up paper in the ends, and put them back on me.

'Better?'

'Um ... think so.'

While my feet were being sorted, another lady dancer was buttoning the borrowed shirt over my borrowed T-shirt. Fortunately no one handed me Leonard's trousers and underwear. The sweat rings under the armpits of the shirt were bad enough. I glanced around for someone – anyone – who might launch some sort of rescue attempt with water pistols at full drench. The first person my eyes hit was PP, standing with Jack and Boz. The cap-wearing flop-head was wearing his fattest grin. He *wanted* me to do this! Why was obvious. He expected me to make a sow's ear of things and give his audience another prize-winning belly-laugh. I slammed my teeth together. Dream on, pal. I was going to dance so well that all he'd get would be the cheers and whistles of the crowd as hats were snatched off and wigs thrown in the air.

'Just go with your instincts, Jimmy,' Carla said. 'Like you did down there.'

We'd just lined up, male types facing female types, and she was opposite me. My dance partner. And that made all the difference. Suddenly, seeing her there, facing me, I was itching to do this.

When the band started up again and our clogs lifted, I was a second or two behind the others, but once I got into it I switched my mind off. I didn't need it. My body knew what to do before my brain did. My arms went up and over, left and right, my legs went every whichway, every rightway, and I stamped my clogs every fourth and sixth beat *perfectly*. I would have been even better if the clogs hadn't been so big. The paper in the toe-caps helped, but my feet still rattled about in them more than I liked. I must have been good enough, though, because when the dance ended the crowd went wild – at my performance.

'You're brilliant, Jimmy!' Carla said.

'Oh, I wouldn't say *brilliant*,' I said modestly.

The other dancers patted me on the back and said nice things too. They didn't seem to mind that I was so good without trying, even though they probably spent all their free time practising. Seemed thrilled to have discovered me actually. One of the female types leaned over me like she was going to kiss me on the cheek, but she can't have seen a clear runway amid the spots because her lips didn't quite land.

When the next dance started I didn't miss a beat from the word go, even though the moves were as complicated and unpredictable as any dance moves

I'd seen anywhere. I'd been pretty good the first time, but this time I was almost as good as the pro dancers, in spite of the too-big clogs.

When this dance ended the eight of us stood still for a bit, soaking up the applause. I gazed around at my adoring fans, wishing I'd practiced my autograph a few more times because they were bound to be queuing for it when we were done. I glanced towards PP. He wasn't grinning now. I was doing something right, very right, which wasn't what he wanted at *all*. I gave him a cheery wave. He did not wave cheerily back.

'Last dance coming up,' one of the troupe told Carla and me. 'It'll be the liveliest, and it gets faster and faster. You might not find it so easy to keep up this time, but don't worry, just have fun.'

I glanced at Carla. She looked a bit worried. I wanted to hug her. Tell her to follow what I did and she'd be all right. But I didn't. Wouldn't have been cool in front of all those people.

The last dance started. They were right about it being livelier. Carla missed a couple of steps a little way in, but I didn't. Even when the rhythm speeded up, my moving parts were just where they needed to be. And as I swayed and twisted and threw my arms about and stamped my big clogs I felt great. On top of the world. I'd found something I was really good at. I mean *really* good.

Soon half the crowd was joining in, or trying to. Wherever you looked, arms were reaching and bodies jerking in all the wrong directions while the eight of us showed them how it should be done. As the music got faster, I got more into it than ever. The band must have noticed this. I saw them look at one another, and nod, then juice the beat even more, which meant that we had to *really* move. And soon –

'I'm out!' Carla shouted, whirling off the platform.

With one less, the even number thing was blown, but the dancing was so frantic now that it didn't seem to matter. The remaining seven of us were just trying to keep up with the beat and one another. In a minute, one of the proper dancers had to drop out too, but the rest of us kept going, and the crowd went berserk. Maybe this was why the band moved up a further gear, which meant that we had to as well. I'd never moved so fast in my life. Never thought I could!

Faster, faster, spin, jump, reach, stamp-stamp,

faster, faster, spin, and … another dancer twirled off the platform.

Only five of us now!

The world was a blur, but somewhere in the blur I caught a glimpse of Carla cheering me on. I couldn't hear her because of the music and the crowd, but I read her gorgeous lips. They were saying, 'Go, Jimmy, go!'

And I went. Boy, did I go, and I never skipped or fluffed a beat until near the end, when I kicked my left leg sky-high and the loose clog on the end of it flew off, and up, almost de-feathering a passing bird. Losing the clog finished me. It wasn't a dance you could do one-clogged. But the fans were still mine. As I jumped off the platform they surged forward to congratulate me, slap me on the back and stuff. And yes, some of them had autograph books.

You'd think PP would have been delighted to see me screw up after all, wouldn't you? But he wasn't. He didn't even stay with Jack while he filmed me failing to finish. He was over at his car by then, jumping up and down with rage. Why? Because my shot clog had zoomed down from the clouds like a meteor and hammered a massive crater in the bonnet of his beloved car, that's why.

Chapter Twenty

By the Tuesday of Week Two, I didn't have just seven spots. My face was all spots. There was still a nose in there somewhere, and a mouth, and a pair of bloodshot eyes, but there were so many fat red lumps that they could have been scatter-painted by a hyperactive two-year-old Jackson Pollock. My face was total Pollocks.

PP, Jack and Boz were still at the house most days, but Carla hadn't appeared since the jamboree. I really missed her, but couldn't help wondering if she was staying away *because* of me. I pictured her lying awake at night thinking of me and hugging her pillow like I was, thinking of her. Maybe PP had noticed the way she looked at me and wouldn't let her come near me as a punishment for clogging his car. I'd apologised for that, but every so often I caught him narrowing his eyes at me. Still, I could handle that. I narrow-eyed him quite a lot when I thought he wasn't looking too.

On the morning of the fourth day before I parted company with the Next Family, Roo, Jess and I were sitting in the kitchen talking to PP about a couple of scenes he still needed to shoot before the end of the week, when Jess asked if we could wear whatever we liked to the party.

'Oh, don't worry about the costumes,' PP said. 'We'll have a rummage through our wardrobe department on your behalf.'

Jess goggle-eyed him. 'Wardrobe department? You mean we'll get to wear costumes that actors have worn on TV?'

'You will.'

Roo and Jess made chuffed noises at this, but I didn't. Not only had I forgotten that there was going to be a party at the end of the shoot, I'd double-forgotten that it was to be a fancy dress one. I groaned.

'What?' Jess said to me.

'I hate fancy dress parties. I mean I *hate* fancy dress parties!'

'Oh, but they're fun,' said Roo.

'Not for me. I hate even putting unfamiliar underpants on, but Vulcan ears or a cowboy suit with a plastic gun?' I pulled a face.

'Maybe they could find you some outfit with a mask,' Roo said.

'A mask?'

'Face mask. Then no one would know it's you. DD?'

PP spread his hands. 'No problem.'

A mask. Yes. It could be anyone behind a mask. Plus – and this was a *big* plus – the millions of viewers would be denied the thrill of seeing the single huge oozing spot that my head was bound to have turned into by then.

'Who'll be at this party?' I asked PP.

'Everyone,' said he of the floppy hair and phoney tan.

'Everyone? You mean every Pole and Armenian, every Swede and German, the entire population of mainland China?'

He managed to curl his lip at me while showing his teeth so the others would think he was grinning at my terrific sense of humour. 'I mean your friends and neighbours, any teachers who can make it, everyone you know and a few you probably didn't know you knew.'

'Any celebrities?' Jess asked hopefully.

'You *are* the celebrities,' said PP.

'We are?'

'You three, your dad, your brother Toby, Jimmy's parents. It'll be some party.'

PP and the crew took that afternoon off, so Jess asked her mum if she would take her into town to meet some friends. When Jess went upstairs to get ready I asked Roo if I would be allowed to go to town too. She said she couldn't see why not and asked where I wanted to be dropped off.

'Well, if you know any good cliffs,' I said.

She frowned. 'Something wrong, Jiggy?'

I sighed. 'These spots. They're worse than ever.'

'Are you using the cream I gave you?'

'Yes, twice a day like it says on the jar.'

'And washing your face between applications?'

'No. Should I?'

'Probably. I suggest that you wash the old cream off before each fresh application. And put it on three times a day, see if that makes a difference.'

Before we went to town I washed my lumpy face very carefully and slapped on more rhino testicle with crossed fingers (difficult). Roo dropped Jess and me off at the shopping centre and Jess went to meet her pals. It wasn't until I was alone that I realised that I'd left my rose pin on the bedside table. I was annoyed. When I wore it I felt like I was carrying a little bit of Carla with me. Felt quite lonely without it actually. I needed company. I thumbed Pete's number.

'Hey, Garrett,' I said when he picked up.

'Hey yourself. You escape again?'

'Yeah. Wanna meet?'

'Nah.'

'What do you mean, "Nah"?'

'I mean I'm busy.'

'Doing what?'

'Toby's coming round.'

'Oh yeah, what for?'

'Stuff. Hey Jig, you wouldn't believe what happened.'

'Tell me.'

'Ask Ange.'

And he clicked off without saying goodbye.

I dialled Angie.

'Hey, Ange. Just spoke to Pete. He said something's happened and to ask you about it.'

'Oh, something's happened all right,' she said. 'I've had some good news.'

'Good news?'

'Grandpa Ralph's died.'

'Who?'

'He was my great-grandpa really, but he was always called Grandpa Ralph. He was ninety-two and I haven't seen him much since I was about five.'

'Why is it good news that he's died?'

'He left me some stuff. There was this note that said he hoped I'd appreciate it because his son and grandson – my dad – never showed much interest.'

'What did he leave you?'

'An old suit of armour.'

'Really?'

'Yes. It came yesterday in a box like a big coffin. You can wear it too.'

'The coffin?'

'The suit. I tried bits of it on, but it's too big for me. Also too big for Pete, but Toby bet him he couldn't wear it for two hours straight this afternoon.'

'Unbelievable,' I said.

'Yeah, well, you know Pete, never can refuse a bet or dare.'

'No, I mean why can't people die and leave me things like that?'

'Since when were you interested in armour?'

'Since when were you?' I said.

'Since yesterday.'

Now *she* clicked off without saying goodbye.

I stared at the phone, unable to believe that my two best buds were too busy with a swapped kid to spare *their* best bud the time of day. It made me very sad. And even more lonely. I wondered who else to call. I thought of Milo Dakin, but if I phoned him his dad might answer, and his dad is Face-Ache Dakin, our form tutor, who really lives up to his name most of the time. There were one or two others – Ian Pitwell, Sami Safadi, Ubik Sprinz, a couple more maybe – but they weren't *best* buds, and they'd've been full of questions about Kid Swap, and I'd had enough of that already without talking about it.

I thought about heel-and-toeing it over to the estate and skimming past my house to see what I could see, but I didn't really want to do that either, so I ended up just wandering around the shopping centre. I looked in some windows – Zappa's Joke Shop, the record shop, a few others – and was ultra bored in zero time. I would have bought myself some fruit, but I'd come out without any lucre, so that was that. Short of nicking something off the stall in front of the fruit and veg shop in the arcade I was destined to remain fruitless for another day – and you wouldn't *believe* how much that made me want some.

When I'd run out of shops and things to be bored by I went into the library to be bored there for a change. It was the usual scene. Kids on computers, Golden Oldies browsing among the few remaining books, an old hobo in a knitted hat snoring in an armchair with the local paper over his face. I glanced at the big news on the front of the hobo's paper. Story about a cat some firemen had rescued from a tree. The woman the cat belonged to was so grateful that she invited the men in for a cuppa. When they'd had the tea they backed the fire truck out of her drive and flattened the mog. The woman was suing the fire service for catslaughter.

After the library I mooched around the edge of the shopping centre, where there are trees for dogs to cock their legs against and a wall for people to spray 'strong language' on. When I saw a couple of boys I knew coming my way I jumped into a passing doorway before they saw me – and crashed into someone coming out.

'Jimmy!'

Carla. My mouth did a goldfish impression for a while before it managed to stammer something about wondering where she'd been since Saturday.

'I've been busy at your house,' she said. 'With Toby and your parents.'

'Oh, I thought you were…'

'Thought I was what?'

'Um … avoiding me?'

I tried to make it sound like a joke, but I'm not sure it worked. I couldn't help thinking of the way my face must look to her.

'It wasn't my choice,' she said, quietly like it was confidential. 'After what happened at the jamboree, DD decided that I was having an unsettling influence on you and told me to keep my distance for a while.'

'Unsettling influence?'

'He thinks I got you a bit overexcited.'

'It wasn't you, it was the music. I was just trying to keep up with it. And my clogs were too big.'

'Yes, I know that,' she said. 'But… well, DD…'

Someone shoved past us to get inside the building, which made me notice for the first time where we were. The doorway belonged to a pub called The Sozzled Sailor. I asked what she was doing there.

She said she'd been having a birthday drink.

'Birthday drink?' I said. 'It's your birthday?'

'Yes. My twenty-third.'

'Your twenty-th...'

My tongue skidded to a slow halt. She was twenty-three? How could she be twenty-three? She didn't *look* twenty-three. And there was I thinking all this time that she was seventeen, eighteen at the most. Seventeen or eighteen made her a bit old for me, but twenty-*three*?! I tried not to look or sound stunned by the news.

'Congratulations. So you were celebrating. On your own?'

'No, with DD.'

'DD?'

'He stopped off at the gents on the way out.'

As she said this the door behind her opened and out he came. He looked surprised to see me for a sec, but then he switched on the smarmy grin that seemed to charm everyone but me and my dad.

'Jimmyyyy.'

The way he said it. Like it was a word that had trouble squeezing between his lips.

'Pee-Peee,' I said, as close to the same way as I could make it.

'It's DD,' said he.

'Yes,' I said. 'And it's Jiggy.'

'Jiggy?'

'Forget it. You have so far, why start getting it right... now?'

There was a pause between 'right' and 'now' because he'd just done something that drove an ice-pick into my heart and out the other side. Put an arm round Carla's shoulders! Then, making sure that I was watching, he pulled her to him and gave her a big fat kiss on the cheek.

And she didn't seem to mind!

In fact she put arm round his waist!

I did the gulping goldfish routine again, which stretched his grin even further. He knew he was making me jealous, and he was tickled rigid.

'Wish I'd known you were sneaking off to a pub,' he said. 'I'd have made sure Jack was here to film you.' He glanced at Carla. 'How come we didn't know?'

She looked at the front of my jacket. 'He's not wearing the pin.'

He also looked at my jacket. 'Why aren't you wearing the pin?'

'Pin?' I said.

'The bug. The tracking gizmo.'

'The tra...'

And I got it. All at once. In a second. Like a slap round the ear. The pin that Carla had given me wasn't a token of affection. It was a gadget that threw out a signal they could follow. No wonder they'd trailed me to the ruined chapel and the orchard!

'So you thought you'd try and con the landlord that you're old enough to drink, did you?' PP said. 'You'll never pull it off, son. You're thirteen and you look it, especially with that juvenile skin complaint.'

Normally when someone says something like that to me I flip a smart one-liner back at them, but the news of Carla's age, plus seeing her and PP with their arms round one another, and finally hearing about the gift that wasn't, had temporarily robbed me of the power of speech. But I must have made some sort of sound deep in my throat that DD didn't like because he leaned towards me, all tight-faced and hard.

'You want to be nice to me, Jimmy boy. I'm editing your episode next week. You're not looking too fabulous as it is, but with a little tweaking you could come over as a badly-co-ordinated teenage Freddie Kruger.'

'Leave him alone, DD, he's only a kid.'

My eyes flicked from his face to Carla's. Only a kid? Only a *kid*?! Suddenly I saw it all. She'd never been interested in me. I was just a boy who had to be coaxed into doing things for her boss's show. Her *boyfriend's* show. An uncooperative brat she'd planted a bug on so they'd know where I was at all times and could be there to film me doing prattish things that were worth their weight in film.

I whirled round.

And ran.

I was still running when I got to the Next house. I ran in the front door, which was open because Mrs Moult was cleaning the brass knocker. I ran up to my room, to my bedside table. I grabbed the rose pin, ran into the en-suite, threw it in the toilet. I pressed the flusher and waited. When the flush died the pin was still there, on the bottom of the pan. I waited and flushed again. The pin stayed. It wasn't going anywhere. Well, I thought, if it won't flush away they'll know where to find me next time they follow the signal, won't they?

In the toilet!

Chapter Twenty-one

Even though I now washed my face between each application of Roo's cream my spots were worse the following day, and worse still the day after that. Whatever it did for Toby Next's spots, extract of rhino testicle did nothing for the McCue variety. I wasn't happy. But PP was. He loved the way I looked. While I was walking around smelling of Bryan Ryan's armpits, face erupting in all directions like a landscape of mini volcanoes, he was hugging himself with glee. I was just what the director ordered. A stinking teenage scowlbot.

The novelty of the Sans-earthist food had worn off pretty much by the end of the week. I'd started to think that it would be years before I'd be able to face anything else off the bone, wing or fin, however tasty the sauce that drowned it. And I was developing an unnatural craving for vegetables. Cabbage! I longed for it. Broccoli! Couldn't wait. Parsnips! I licked my lips. Peas, swede, green beans, lettuce, celery – I thought I would die if I didn't soon gorge myself on all of them, cooked, raw, washed, or thick with dirt, riddled with worms.

At last the Kid Swap shoot came to an end. My ordeal was almost over. All I had to do now was get through the fancy dress party and I'd be back in my own bed, a carrot in one hand, a sprout in the other.

PP unveiled our fancy dress costumes just an hour before the party. He gave Roo a Cleopatra costume, Solomon a Captain Jack Sparrow, and Jess a Hippy Chick (flowery flares, tasselled waistcoat, headband, long wig). Jess was told to put on heavy eye make-up and go around in a daze waving a couple of fingers and saying, 'Peace, man'.

The only one of us who wasn't thrilled with his fancy dress was me. PP had said he would get me a costume with a mask, and he did. A super-hero costume. Fine, you might say. Just the job. Think Spiderman, think Judge Dread, think Iron Man. No chance of guessing the features behind *their* masks. But PP didn't bring me a costume like that. The mask of the one he gave me wasn't even a half-face-coverer like Batman's. No, the mask of the totally unknown superhero the wally-brain had picked out for me only just covered my eyes. Even my eyebrows rose above it (quite a long way actually, when I saw myself in it). And it had these little red blobs all over it. Little red blobs almost identical to the ones that covered the space between my hairline and chin and all points east and west between my ears.

And the rest of the costume? You had to see it to believe it. It was all droopy and saggy, and it had these fake arm and leg muscles and a little cape, and, like the mask, it was a riot of red blobs from head to toe. There were even a couple on the nipples, which stood out like corks that had spent the afternoon in a pencil sharpener. There was a hat too. A helmet sort of thing, with a red teat on top that wobbled as I shook with horror. Standing in front of a full-length mirror it was hard to tell where the spots on me ended and the spots on the costume began. I was the hero the world had not been waiting for: Spot Man!

'What…?' I said, eyes popping through the little mask at my reflection.

'What what?' said PP, who was standing by with his hand over his mouth.

'…is it supposed to be?' I managed.

'It's a costume from a wacky super-hero sitcom that'll be transmitted in September. You'll be giving the world a sneak preview, Jim. Don't you feel privileged?'

'Privileged?' I cried. '*Privileged?* Why have you *done* this?'

He screwed his eyes up at me. 'Because this is TV, my son, and the audience will wet themselves when they see you in that.' He turned to go, but then turned back, and winked at me. 'You didn't think I'd forgotten what you did to my car, did you?'

Unlike me, Jess was quite excited about the party. With the thick eye make-up, headband and wig she looked like a different person, which I guess was the idea.

'It's all right for you,' I said when she told me how much she was looking forward to the evening. 'You're not going as Captain Boil.'

'Relax,' she said. 'It's only a party.'

'Relax? In *this*?'

'You'll be wearing it for an hour or two at most. No time at all. Just look at it as the last thing you have to get through before going back to your family.'

'I can't wait,' I said, feeling one of my huge lumpy muscles. 'And I never thought I'd say *that* this side of my tenth lifetime.'

'Jiggy,' she said. 'Haven't you enjoyed anything about the past two weeks?'

'Er… Toby's en-suite?'

'Is that all?' She looked a bit hurt by this. 'I thought it was fun.'

'Might've been for you,' I whinged. 'You didn't get caught on camera doing stupid things all the time.'

'Well, I hope Toby had a better time at your place.'

'Even if he didn't, I bet they didn't make him wear anything like this.'

And they hadn't. When we got to the town hall where the party was to occur we saw Toby dressed as a paratrooper. In his tin helmet and camouflage he looked pretty ordinary beside me. *Everyone* looked ordinary beside me.

'Jiggy?'

I turned. 'No,' I said to the pregnant bunny girl with the floppy ears.

'It's me – Mum.'

'Really? Hey, those fishnet stockings had me fooled.' I looked her up and down, wincing every inch of the way, partly because I'd never seen my mother look so ridiculous, partly because I hadn't had any plans to ever see another rabbit. 'I suppose your director chum chose that,' I said.

'He did. Personally.' She sounded quite proud of this. 'Between you and me, I think DD fancies me.'

She went all coy as she said this. I gazed at her with pity.

'Mother, you're seven months preggers, and it shows. I mean it *really* shows. If someone fancied you, do you actually think they'd stick you in a thing as itsy as that, with a cottonwool tail, foot-long ears, and boobs pumped up to your chin?'

She laughed. 'I'm a bunny girl, Jiggy. This is a traditional bunny girl costume.' Now she took a turn at looking me up and down. 'Yours is very amusing.'

'Amusing?' I said. 'Oh, *that's* the word I've been searching for.'

'And that make-up. The artificial spots. Perfect match for the pattern on the costume.'

I let it go. I didn't want to *think* about my face, let alone discuss it. To change the subject I asked my mother if there was anything left in her veggy patch at home. She said of course there was and why did I want to know. I admitted that I was kind of starved of veg. She looked around for something to clutch on the way to her knees.

'You're what?'

'I'll explain later. What was it like having another kid living with you?'

She pulled herself together and at the same time went all misty-eyed.

'Oh, Toby's such an attractive boy. And so good-natured, so easy to get on with. We've grown rather attached to him.'

'More attached to him than me?'

'You?' she said, like she'd forgotten for a minute who I was. But then she remembered. 'Don't be silly, darling, you're our son.'

'Doesn't mean you have to like me more than him.'

'Jiggy,' she said, coming over all serious.

'Mother,' said I, as seriously as I could while dressed as Ultra Prat.

'Even though you're a bit hard-going sometimes, even though you can be a real pain, your dad and I will always love you more than anyone else. At least until your baby sister arrives.'

'Did he eat his fruit and veg?' I asked.

'Who?'

'Toby.'

'Yes, without a *word* of complaint. Why?'

'He didn't say anything?'

'What about?'

I shook my head. So even though Toby didn't eat the things at home because his family thought they were contaminated, he'd swallowed them at my house without even saying he shouldn't. That kid was just too good to be true.

I looked around the big hall. 'Where's my father?'

'See if you can pick him out,' Mum said.

The hall was crammed with weirdly-dressed people by this time, and getting more crammed every minute. I recognised a lot of the costumes, but not so many of the people inside them. I certainly couldn't identify my father. Mum pointed to two fancily-dressed types standing by a radiator.

'Count Dracula?' I said.

'The one next to him.'

The one next to Count D was a big yellow fluffy creature with enormous feet, huge round eyes, long beak, and a wavy red crest standing up on its head. I cleared my throat.

'What's... what's he meant to be?'

'A cock,' Mum said.

'A *what*?'

'A cockerel. Male chicken.'

'I'm betting that that was our favourite director's choice too.'

'Of course. He kitted out all three of us.' She giggled. 'Your dad says he's never felt such a herbert. Serve him right for being such a misery these past two weeks.'

'Jig!'

I turned towards the new voice, to face Betty Boop and a suit of ancient armour.

'Who's your rusty friend?' I said to Betty (Angie).

One of the suit of armour's hands clanked upward and tried to raise the visor. A muffled voice spoke from somewhere inside. I asked Angie what he'd said.

'Dunno. Can't make out a word. The top of his head's somewhere around the chin. What are you s'posed to be anyway?'

'That has yet to be decided,' I said.

'What's with the posh talk?'

'Posh talk?'

'"That has yet to be decided".'

'What else would I say?'

'Well *normally* you'd say something like "Whaddayathink I'm supposed to be, the Leaning Tower of Pizza?" Sounds like you've got above yourself since you got your own en-suite and pool.'

'Well, I'll be back with you peasants after tonight,' I said. 'That'll bring me back down to earth.'

'I'll leave you three to catch up,' said Mum.

'Cool outfit, Peg,' said Angie as my mother turned away.

'Thanks, Ange!' said the bunny girl with the Mount Vesuvius tum. She waddled off, waggling her fish-netted bum cheeks and little white tail.

I heard a squealy thud from my side. Pete had got the visor up. When he stretched his neck inside the suit of armour you could just see his eyes in the lower part of the gap.

'Whew,' he said. 'And they used to *fight* in these things?'

'They were grown men,' Angie said, 'not the runts of the litter.'

'I thought they were shorter in those days.'

'Not as short as you, obviously.'

'You look like a giant germ,' Garrett said to me.

'Or something out of a panto that got cancelled halfway through the first night.' (Angie Boop.)

'Pus in boots.' (Garrett.)

'Super-pus.' (Angie.)

'Do you two mind not talking about the way I look?' (Me.)

'Sure,' said Pete. 'But boy, do you look stupid.'

'I know I look stupid. I also know that my mum and dad look stupid. That means that every McCue in town looks stupid. But the Next Family? Oh, no. They look pretty normal for people in fancy dress. I could kill PP.'

'PP?' said Angie.

'The director. He really has it in for us.'

'Ooh, there's someone I haven't seen in a while,' Sir Pete said suddenly.

We followed his gaze. He was looking at empty space.

'Who?' I asked.

'The Invisible Man. Catch you later.'

'He doesn't change,' I said to Ange as Pete clunked off like a very heavy marionette.

'Slow developer.' She turned back to me. 'Your make-up's pretty convincing. Those spots look like they're really weeping.'

'They are weeping.'

'What do you mean?'

'I mean they're not make-up. They're real.'

'Real?'

'All mine.' I did not say this proudly.

'You mean since we last met your seven spots have turned into...'

She started counting. I stopped her.

'Can we just say there's a few more and change the subject?'

'A *few*!' she said. 'And they're so *horrible*! I've never seen so many disgusting spots on one face. God, Jig, what have you been *doing*?'

'Nothing.'

'Oh, come *on*. No one could get so many hideous growths in so short a time without doing something they don't usually do.'

'The only thing I can think of is the food,' I said.

She asked what food and I told her about the meals the Next Family ate, and the lunchtime pills.

'In that case,' she said, 'I'm not surprised you look so repulsive. Well, I am, a bit. I mean, any average person who ate nothing but rubbish for a couple of weeks would just get a bit blotchy or pale. But you? Bang over the top as usual.'

'Thanks for the support,' I said miserably.

My mood wasn't lightened by the old-style rock music that started leaking out of speakers hidden in plastic ferns on the walls. People in fancy dress

219

immediately started wiggling about and waving their arms.

'Ooh, time to dance,' Angie said. 'With someone *normal*.'

She scampered away to find a dance partner. Grabbed a tall flat-headed person with a green face and a bolt through his neck. She thought he was normal compared to me. Now that *was* depressing.

Chapter Twenty-two

Jack and another cameraman were filming everything that moved, so I backed into an alcove. From there I took in all the fancy dress through my useless mask. There were genies and penguins and Jedi knights, and gorillas and gangsters and tramps, and Talking Mice and Bilbos and Peter Pans, and angels and devils, and bears and wizards, and – well, you name it there was someone dressed that way. I saw Carla too. She was one of the few – along with PP, Jack, Boz, and the other cameraman and his assistant – who weren't dressed up to look like someone else or some creature or thing. She saw me and waved, then turned away. Next week she'd be working on something else and I'd be history. I was nearly that already. I noticed for the first time the way she looked at other blokes and was amazed I hadn't seen it before. The big eyes, the warm toothy smile, the arm-touching. She wasn't being sly. She wasn't flirting, not really. It was just her way. But every man or boy she did it to lapped it up and went all saggy-jawed. Just like I had.

A couple of my teachers were among the guests. One was my Pointless Exercises teacher, Mr Rice. The other was Mr Dent, the Resistant Materials honcho. I'm not a massive fan of Mr Rice, but you can have a laugh with Mr Dent, and you know (because he's said) that he'd rather be playing in his rock band than showing kids how to resist materials. It was one of the few times that I'd seen Mr Rice in anything but a red tracksuit. Tonight he was dressed as an old-style gangster – black-and-white striped suit, white tie, black hat, violin case. And Mr Dent? He was running on the spot in trainers, blowing a sporty whistle, wearing a red tracksuit. Mr Rice glared at him like he wanted to mow him down with his violin.

I noticed the big male chicken who used to be my father talking to my barrel-tummed bunny mother. She pointed to my alcove and his enormous feet flapped towards me. He was a pretty sad sight across the room, but up close he looked even raggeder and droopier.

'Hi, Dad.'

The big round eyes stared. 'How'd you know it was me?'

'I'd know those feathers anywhere.'

'I can't believe I'm wearing this,' he said through his beak.

'Same here, you and me both.'

'Those blobs on your face are a nice touch. The way they match the ones on the outfit.'

'Yeah. Your feathers are a nice touch too, the way they match your brain. I'm surprised you even left the house in that.'

'It was your mum. She threatened to throw a moody if I didn't shut my beak and put up with it.'

'She couldn't look much more ridiculous either,' I said.

He agreed. 'But DD told her she looked sexy and she believed him. God, that man, I'd like to...'

'Yes?'

'Never mind. Soon be over. See you later.'

With that he left me, flapping his big feet and waggling his wings like any other giant cock.

I was still loitering in the alcove wondering how long this thing would go on for when my mother returned – not in such a jolly mood this time.

'Angie tells me those spots are real,' she said as a volcano on my cheek erupted. She wiped her shoulder with one of her bunny ears.

'Oh, they're real all right,' I said.

'You didn't say.'

'You didn't ask.'

'How did your face get that way?'

'I'm guessing it was the food.'

'Food? What food?'

'The Next Family eat different rubbish to us.'

'It can't be that different. Their faces are clear.'

'Yeah, but they're used to not eating fruit and veg.'

'They don't eat fruit and vegetables?'

'No.'

'What – ever?'

I shook my head. My super-helmet with the teat on top wobbled. 'They believe that anything that comes out of the earth is bad for you.'

'So you've had no fruit or vegetables the whole time you've been away?'

'No.'

She was shocked. I mean really shocked. 'Jiggy,' she said. 'If I'd known you were going to be denied decent food for an entire fortnight I would never have let you take part in the series.'

'They knew that. You were set up. I tried to tell you they'd pull something, but would you listen?'

'Set up?'

'By the TV company. PP.'

'PP?'

'DD. He knew the Next Family didn't eat f and v, and that you made me. He wanted to see how me and Toby would adjust to different eating arrangements. Toby ate things he never does at home and I didn't. Never *ever* thought I'd miss that stuff, but holy onions, I could use a leek!'

'There's a toilet in the corridor.' (She was only half listening.)

'I tell you, Mum, if one of these people was dressed as a boxer I'd bite his cauliflower ear off. I almost sank my teeth into that person dressed as a red pepper just now.'

'That would have been vegicide,' said a passing Homer Simpson.

'You really believe that DD knew Toby's family would be denying you the nourishment I insist upon?' my mother asked.

'Ask him yourself if you don't believe me. You never know, he might come clean as it's the last day.'

Her eyes shrank to the size of pin-heads. I knew those eyes very well. You can push the old dear quite a way – I do it all the time, it's a sort of hobby – but there's a point when you know you've gone too far. When that happens the best thing you can do is cover your privates until her sad Golden Oldie brain forgets what she was talking about and she shifts the subject to hair or shoes or something.

Now Mum's pin-heads were searching the room. They found the person she wanted, directing the camera action as Jack filmed a group of jiving garden gnomes. She set off towards him without another word, her little tail bobbing in the breeze. I went after her. On the way I passed my father having a conversation about politics with a stick of rock.

'What's up?' he said as I went by.

'I think Mum's a tad upset with our director.'

'*Her* upset with *him*? What's he done?'

'Made me come out in spots.'

'The costume?'

'The face.'

'It's only make-up,' he said.

I laughed, and walked on. By the time I caught up with Mum she was talking to PP, and her voice was rising.

'Are you admitting, DD, actually *admitting*, that

you knew he wouldn't be eating proper food for the entire two weeks?'

'It's proper food to the Nexts,' he replied, smooth as treacle.

'Have you seen what their diet's done to his skin?'

DD chuckled. 'He'll look a treat on the box, full colour, wide-screen. With the trailers showing him like that, you as a pregnant bunny girl, and Mel as a cockerel, we'll get some of the highest ratings of the week. You'll have 'em rolling in the aisles.'

'Rolling in the...' My mother took a breath. 'You mean you expect people to laugh at us?'

'If they don't I haven't done my job. You'll be the toast of the tabloids. They'll want your life stories. You'll be invited to appear on Celebrity Russian Roulette. Get some snaps of Mel with some inflated floozy and you could get a ghost-written best-seller out of it.'

Mum bit her bunny lip. 'So it's true,' she murmured.

'What is?'

'What Jiggy said. That you set us up.'

'Setting people up is what shows like Kid Swap are all about, love,' PP said. (Suddenly she was 'love' and the charm was off. Now he was a fake-tanned wide-boy with floppy hair and mocking eyes.) 'The material we have of you three is so good we're gonna fast-track the edits and put your ep out first to launch the series.'

'So…'

Mum paused, eyes half closed, mind churning silently. I could almost see what was going through it. Her family was dressed like this and her son had become a freak because this man knew it was a way to get viewers. Somewhere in the distance, a mass of heavy metal hit parquet. Sir Pete d'Garrett had toppled over, face first. My mother was one of the few who didn't seem to hear. She was still trying to get her head round this new angle when I felt something large and soft (but not cuddly) come to stand beside me. My feathered father.

'Don't you worry your pretty little tummy about it, darling,' PP said, putting his hands on Mum's shoulders and becoming a full-frontal Mr Oilypants. 'You'll be a riot. I wouldn't be surprised if you won me a Bafta.'

Mum's mind snapped out of its trance and she stepped back sharply. PP's hands fell away.

'Clearly you're not the person I took you for,' she said. 'But now that I see what you've been up to…'

PP shoved his hands in his pockets. He was smiling the smile of someone who's pleased with himself and doesn't care who knows it.

'Now that you see what I've been up to...?'

'We're pulling out.'

'What?'

'Of the series.'

He chuckled. 'Can't do it, sweetheart. Signed a contract, remember?'

'Well I'm breaking it,' said Mum.

A spot of fake tan drained from PP's cheeks, but he did his best to keep the trademark smirk in place.

'If you did that the company would have to sue you, I'm afraid.'

She grabbed me and hugged me to her. 'Not before I sued you for what you did to my son.'

'*I* didn't do anything,' PP said, flicking a glance of hatred my way.

'But you're to blame. You and your company. You deliberately lodged him with a household that consumes non-nourishing foods and you've admitted that you expected something like this to happen. I have witnesses.'

She waved around at Mr Bean, Mr Toad, a fairy and a hobbit, all well tuned in to every word.

There were nods and mutters of agreement.

'Nice one, Peg,' clucked the cock at my side.

PP seemed to be getting the idea now, but he wasn't going to roll over just like that. The smirk stayed on his face.

'You can't pull out at this late stage,' he said. 'We've been filming for two full weeks. We've spent tens of thousands on you.'

'Then you're going to lose tens of thousands,' Mum said.

'And you won't get your fee.'

'Stuff the fee.'

His smirk finally dipped. 'What?'

'And stuff you.'

With this, my mother whirled away, hauling one of my bulging super-hero arms with her. The rest of me went along for the ride, but when I looked back I saw that Dad had stayed put. He was leaning towards PP, tapping him on the chest with one of his claws.

'What about the money?' I asked Mum as we went.

'Money?'

'That they were going to pay you for Kid Swap.'

'We'll manage.'

'How?'

'I'll find your dad a job. And as for you…'

'Me?'

'You can do something part-time.'

I groaned. But not too loudly. I was going home.
To fresh fruit and veg!

Chapter Twenty-three

The Next Family were pretty good about us walking out on Kid Swap. Sad about losing the publicity they would have got for Sans-earthism, but understanding. They even apologised to Mum for not giving me the nourishment she thought I needed. Roo and Jess said I could come over any time I wanted to use the pool. I said if I did I'd bring my own trunks, not an elephant's. We had a good laugh about that.

'They seem far too nice to hold such extremist views,' Mum said after our last meeting with them.

'Yeah, they're OK,' I said.

When the news got around that we'd given the TV company the elbow, Bryan Ryan said we were chicken ('Tell my dad that,' I said to him), but Eejit Atkins thought it was kind of cool and that he'd swap his brother Jolyon for me any time – good of him seeing as Jolyon, with his tattoos and attitude and all, is a darkside hero of his.

A few weeks after the walk-out the doorbell rang.

It was Pete and Angie. They had the free local paper with them.

'Have you seen this?' Pete asked when Mum brought them through to the kitchen, where I was making a vegetable stew from a recipe book.

I told them that the free paper hadn't been rammed through our letter flap since Dad fixed a notice to the gate saying that hawkers, Mormons and timewasters weren't welcome. Now even the milk wasn't delivered.

'Well as it happens it's about your dad,' said Angie.

'What is?' I asked.

'He's in here. He's famous.'

I wiped my hands on my apron and snatched the paper. It wasn't a big article, but there was a photo with it – of someone in a chicken costume. Mum looked over my shoulder.

'We'll never live this down,' she said.

'It's a different costume,' I said. 'Look. The bit on top's wrong and the beak's not as long. They probably hired it specially because they didn't have a pic of Dad in his. He has to see this.'

'He can see it when he gets home,' said Mum.

'No, I have to show him now. Might cheer him up.'

'You don't know where he's been deployed today.'

'I do. He phoned earlier to moan about it. He's litter-picking at the Really Golden Oldie Home that I've just put your names down for.'

I rolled the newspaper up and shot off with it before P & A could invite themselves along. I didn't want anyone else there when I showed my dad the article. This was family stuff.

When I got to the Arnold Snit Retirement Home I found him in the grounds with a loaded wheelbarrow.

'I've learnt something today, Jig,' he said when I joined him.

'What's that then?'

'That it's not only you kids who don't know what rubbish bins are for. Stacks of bins here, but most of the crap goes straight on the ground. If it was up to me, I'd make them get down on their knees and pick it up themselves. Still,' he added, 'it's better than yesterday, scrubbing the graffiti off the Ladies in the shopping centre. Long job. What brings you here?'

'Thought you'd like to see this.'

I opened the paper. He leaned over to look at it.

MY FEATHERS WERE RUFFLED, SAYS CHICKEN MAN

A 43-year-old unemployed man accused of bird-brained behaviour was today sentenced to a month's Community Service for assaulting television director Darius Drane while dressed as a chicken. According to bystanders Incredible Hulk and Goldilocks, Melvyn Dudley McCue went after Mr Drane wing and claw. At the hearing, McCue claimed that Mr Drane had ruffled his feathers during the making of a TV series in which they were both involved. In sentencing him, the beak, Mr Justice Grain-Harker said, 'Such fowl behaviour cannot be condoned in this day and age.'

Dad frowned. 'I wasn't a chicken, I was a cock.'

'Probably a good thing they didn't know that,' I said.

'The picture's not even of me.'

But he was quite chuffed that he'd been noticed, and later, when he came home, he said he was going to frame the article.

'Name and picture in the paper,' he said. 'And *without* appearing on that stinking show.'

'Not you in the picture,' I reminded him.

'It is as far as anyone else is concerned, and that's good enough.'

Mum was less pleased about the publicity than he was.

'If Pinocchio and Widow Twankey hadn't hauled you off in time,' she said, 'you might have pecked DD's eyes out. Then you'd have been put away for a very long time.'

'You'd have been a jailbird,' I said.

For tea that night we had the stew I made earlier. I was getting good at veggie cooking, though as usual Dad complained about the lack of meat in it. It wasn't the weekend, but we had the stew on trays in front of the telly because there was something we wanted to see.

The first episode of Kid Swap.

It was awful, highly embarrassing, and you couldn't help feeling sorry for some of the people in it, but it gave us a laugh or two. Why? Why do you think? Because we were among the millions watching others make todgers of themselves – not the ones providing the entertainment!

Jiggy McCue

(Almost-Famous-TV-Celeb)

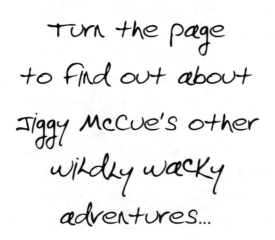

978 1 86039 836 0 £4.99

Something's after Jiggy McCue!
Something big and angry and invisible.
Something which hisses and flaps and stabs
his bum and generally tries to make
his life a misery. Where did it come from?

Jiggy calls together the Three Musketeers
– One for all and all for lunch! –
and they set out to send the poltergoose
back where it belongs.

Shortlisted for the Blue Peter Book Award

The underpants from hell – that's what
Jiggy calls them, and not just because they
look so gross. No, these pants are evil.
And they're in control. Of him. Of his life!
Can Jiggy get to the bottom of his
problem before it's too late?

"...the funniest book I've ever read."
Teen Titles

"Hilarious!"
The Independent

Winner of the Stockton Children's
Book of the Year Award

orchard Red Apples

Other Jiggy McCue books by Michael Lawrence:

Orchard books are available from all good bookshops, or can be ordered direct from the publisher:
Orchard Books, PO BOX 29, Douglas IM99 1BQ
Credit card orders please telephone: 01624 836000 or fax: 01624 837033
or visit our website: www.orchardbooks.co.uk or e-mail: bookshop@enterprise.net for details.

To order please quote title, author and ISBN and your full name and address.
Cheques and postal orders should be made payable to 'Bookpost plc.'
Postage and packing is FREE within the UK (overseas customers should add £1.00 per book).

Prices and availability are subject to change.